GW00789037

A GOOSE ON YOUR GRAVE

A GOOSE
ON YOUR GRAVE

Joan Aiken

LONDON
VICTOR GOLLANCZ LTD
1987

First published in Great Britain 1987
by Victor Gollancz Ltd,
14 Henrietta Street, London WC2E 8QJ

Copyright © Joan Aiken Enterprises Ltd 1987

British Library Cataloguing in Publication Data
Aiken, Joan
   A goose on your grave.
   I. Title
   823'.914[J]   PZ7

   ISBN 0-575-03985-X

Photoset and printed in Great Britain by
WBC Print Ltd, Bristol

Contents

Your Mind is a Mirror

A keen wind scoured the deck of the ferryship *Colossos*, probing between the slats of the wooden seats on the upper section, making the passengers huddle together, pull on cardigans if they had them, or go below for cups of hot coffee. Mist was beginning to veil the Turkish coast on the left-hand side, and blur the shapes of the islands to the right. Another hour must pass before the ship docked in Rhodes. Sam and Linnet wrapped their bare legs in their swimming towels, but a damp swimming towel is very poor protection against a cold searching wind. They had begged for a last swim and Ma had said, "Oh, very well! Meet us at the dock, and promise you won't be a minute later than half past twelve. But that means you'll have to wear beach clothes on the boat, because your other clothes will be packed."

"Doesn't matter," Sam had said. "It'll be hot."

But it wasn't hot; the weather had turned misty and windy. "Most unlike the Aegean at this time of year," other passengers were grumbling. The Palmers' luggage was at the very bottom of a huge heap of bags and crates on the lower deck; impossible to dig down to their rucksacks and get out warmer clothes. All their books were packed, too; there was nothing to do but sit and shiver, for the boat was jam-packed

7

with tourists, mainly Swedes and Germans—you couldn't even walk about to keep yourself warm, because there wasn't a foot of deck space free. Sam did his best to doze a bit; he had woken very early and listened to the crowing of roosters near and far, anxious not to miss a minute of their last day on Kerimos. But it was too cold on the boat for proper sleeping; he had a brief, sad dream about his beloved French teacher who had died, Madame Bonamy: "Will you carry these books for me, please, Sam," she was saying, "they are too heavy for me, and I brought a coat for you, en effet, I have brought several, as I did not know which one would fit you." In fact she had brought half a dozen coats, every coat he could remember owning since he was five: the navy duffel, the red plastic anorak, the sheepskin-lined blue wool, the green gaberdine raincoat, the yellow slicker, the camel overcoat passed on from Cousin Ted, and the grey suede windcheater he had worn till it fell apart. So he had to carry all those as well as the three heavy boxes of books, and he could hardly stagger along under the load. He woke up with a jerk, just as Madame Bonamy was saying, "Oh, mon Dieu, Sam, but you will have to go back to Kerimos again, because—"

Go *back*, carrying that weight of stuff? Not likely, he thought, and shook himself hurriedly out of sleep. Father was sitting staring ahead in silence, as usual, and Ma was murmuring something to Linnet in a low anxious voice.

In several ways it had been a miserable holiday. The tiny Greek island was beautiful, of course; the little Greek house with its bare painted floors, basic wooden furniture, and garden full of roses and lemons, had been perfect; the swimming in a clear green sea, the cliffs covered with rockroses, the village that was all steps up and steps down, dazzling white houses, ancient crumbling churches, and flowers everywhere—every detail of that had been marvellous,

8

paradisial, but Father had spoiled it. Silent, grim, day after day, he had sat in one place, generally the darkest corner of the darkest room indoors, unless Ma had urged him to go out, when he had shrugged and slouched into the garden, as if it did not matter to him where he moved his load of misery. On excursions, or when they ate dinner at one of the tavernas on the quayside, he had accompanied his wife and children like an angry, speechless ghost. Why should he object if we are enjoying ourselves? thought Sam resentfully. We aren't doing *him* any harm.

Possibly Father didn't really notice whether they were enjoying themselves or not; he never looked at the other three members of his family, just stared off into the distance like an Easter Island statue on the side of a hill. His wife and children shared plain, nondescript looks: Sam and Linnet had straight brown hair, snub noses, freckles and greyish brown eyes; Ma had a pleasant friendly face, but it was always worried nowadays which made it almost ugly; she didn't bother about clothes or make-up much any more, and her hair was badly in need of a perm; it looked like a piece of knitting that had gone wrong. Father had always been the handsome member of the family, with his classically straight forehead and nose, all in one line, his bright brown hair and beard, now just touched with grey, and bright dark twinkling grey eyes. But now his eyes had ceased to twinkle; they stared into the distance, hour after hour, day after day, as if nothing nearby had the power to please them. Once, his conversation had been full of jokes and interesting information; now, often a whole day would pass without his speaking at all except to say, "I don't mind."

"Would you rather have a boiled egg or scrambled, Jonathan?" Ma would ask at breakfast.

"Do you want to watch BBC or ITV?"

"Shall we go to Brighton and see Fanny, or for a walk on the Heath?"

"I don't mind."

In the end, Ma hadn't even bothered to consult him about the holiday on Kerimos; she sold some shares Granny had left her, bought the tickets, rented the house, and packed Father's bag for him. He hadn't raised any objections. But, for all the good that sun and sea and Greek air had done him, he might as well have stayed at home in Camden Town.

"You do realize he's sick, don't you?" Ma had said anxiously to Sam.

"How do you mean, sick? Has he got a pain, is something wrong with him?"

Sickness to Sam meant medicine, hospitals, bandages, injections.

"His mind is sick. He's depressed, because he was made redundant, because he can't get a teaching job anywhere. And he's such a good teacher—"

Sam couldn't see it. Lots of the boys at school had unemployed parents, who grumbled and moaned, of course, worried about money, were hopeful of jobs, or disappointed when the hopes came to nothing, but in between times they seemed reasonably cheerful, mowed their lawns, took the family to the movies once in a way, didn't retreat into this marble staring world of silence. Why did Jonathan Palmer have to be so different?

An extra keen gust of wind worked its way under Sam's thin T-shirt and he shivered.

"Brr, I'm freezing!"

"So am I," sighed Linnet.

Their father's indifferent gaze passed right over them, as if they had spoken in Hindustani, but Ma said, "Here, you two, here's a couple of hundred drachmae. You'd better go and

buy yourselves a coffee. And bring some back for me and
Father. I'll stay here . . ."

"I wonder if she thinks he might jump over the side,"
murmured Linnet, shivering, as they stood in line at the
coffee counter.

Sam muttered, "I hate Dad. I really hate him. I almost
wish he would jump over the side."

"Oh, Sam. You know it's just that he's ill. And think how
hard it must have been for him losing his job, when Ma's still
teaching at the same school. He just isn't himself. Remember!
He never used to be like this."

"Well, why can't he go back to the way he used to be?"
Sam said disbelievingly.

"People can't get better just by wanting to."

"Well, then he ought to go to a shrink."

"Costs money. And the Health Service shrinks have
waiting lists as long as the Milky Way." Linnet paid for the
coffee and looked frustratedly at the huge pile of baggage.
"I do wish we could get out books and read."

Sam fingered the beach satchel under his arm. As well as
damp swimming trunks, flippers and snorkel mask, it
contained a guilty secret.

Several times, swimming from the tiny town beach, they
had noticed a Greek family group who attracted Sam's
attention because they seemed in every way the converse of
the Palmers. There were two lively handsome dark brothers,
older; two small pretty sisters, younger; there was a fat
cheerful aunt, a plump smiling mother, and, above all, there
was a talkative, ebullient father who seemed the king-pin of
the whole tribe—affectionate with the girls, companionable
and teasing with the boys, bounding in and out of the water,
rushing away to the quay and returning with almond cakes,
ice creams and fruit; sweeping the family off to eat lunch at

11

quayside tavernas, and all the time making jokes, laughing, hugging his wife, complimenting his sister-in-law, carrying the smaller girl piggyback up the rocky path. If only Father could be like that! Had he ever been?

Sam could hardly remember the days before Jonathan Palmer's illness; the mist of unhappiness that surrounded him seemed to block out any view of the past.

On this final morning the Greek father had produced from his pocket a little book, a glossy paperback, from which he proceeded to read aloud, amid bursts of general hilarity. At every paragraph, almost every sentence he read, his wife, children and sister-in-law collapsed and beat their chests in hiccups of laughter. Sam could feel a smile break out over his own face at the sight and sound of so much happy humour. Then, gaily, impulsively, forgetting the book, leaving their swimming things scattered on the sand, they had all gone bounding off to the nearest quayside café for coffee and cakes. Linnet was still in the sea, making the most of her last swim, nobody else on the beach was anywhere near; Sam had walked past, casually dropped his towel, and picked up towel and book together. Why? He hardly knew himself. Perhaps the book was a kind of token, a talisman, a spell, a magic text that would bring fun and good humour back into his own family if he read it aloud?

There had been no chance to look inside the book since he picked it up; Linnet had dashed out of the sea, they had dressed and sprinted round to the berth where the *Colossos* waited at her moorings. But now Sam could feel the paperback, a small, encouraging rectangular shape, wrapped in a plastic bag between his trunks and towel. He would study it tonight, when they were back at home; though now it seemed almost impossible to believe that by bedtime they would be in their own house in Camden Town, the island of

12

Kerimos, with its white houses and turquoise sea, nothing but a bright memory.

Home, when they reached it, smelt shut-in and stuffy; Ma went round at once throwing open windows. Father sat down, just as he was, without even pulling off his windcheater, in a chair by the fireplace, and stared, unseeing, at the unlit gas fire. Home smelt of all the sorrow that had ever happened there . . .

But here was fat Simon, Sam's cat; a plump, sharply-striped young tabby, half-frantic with pent-up affection, wanting to be picked up, rolling on his back to have his stomach rubbed, leaping on to Sam's lap at every possible and impossible moment, miaowing and purring nonstop and simultaneously to indicate his displeasure at having been left to the care of neighbours for two solid weeks.

"I don't believe a word of what you say!" Sam told him. "*You* aren't starved, fat cat Simon—you're even fatter than you were when we left. You should see some of those skinny Greek cats, you spoilt thing."

The island had been full of cats, healthy and active but thin as diagrams; they waited hungrily and acrimoniously for fishbones around every quayside café.

Sam raced up to his room with Simon wailing two steps behind him, flung his rucksack on the bed, then pulled the stolen book from his beach satchel and eagerly opened it.

The disappointment was shattering; there were no pictures in the book and (as he might have realized if he had given it a moment's thought) the text was all in Greek, in Greek characters; he could read no more than a word here and there, *kai* for and, *alla* for but. He had committed theft, he had stolen a book, the book that had given them all such joy, and it was no use to him, no use at all. Guilt began to rise up in

13

him like bubbles in jam that has started to ferment and go bad. He felt sick with dismay and horror at what he had done . . .

"Sam, you're tired out," said Ma, looking at him acutely when he came downstairs with a load of dirty clothes for the machine. "Off you go, straight to bed. It's too late for supper. Lin's gone up already."

Father had not gone to bed. He sat on, staring at the dead fire; he often sat that way all night.

"Good night, Father," Sam called, but did not expect, or receive, any answer.

Sam dragged himself up the stairs to bed, feeling as if he had travelled three times, on hands and knees, round the world. His only comfort (but that a substantial one, he must admit) was fat cat Simon, lovingly shoving himself as close to Sam's chin as he could squeeze.

Sam fell asleep and began to dream instantly.

There was Madame Bonamy, half stern, half smiling, as she often had been, her white wild hair standing up in a corona all round her head, elegantly tilted on its long neck, her deepset dark eyes watchful on either side of an aquiline nose, her mouth set in a firm line.

Madame Bonamy had been quite young, in her thirties; illness, not age, had turned her hair white. Her skin was smooth, but completely colourless; that, and the fine thistledown white hair had given her the look of a ghost long before she became one. She did not behave like a ghost, then or in Sam's dreams. As a teacher she had been very funny, used to tell zany, crazy stories, and dry, ironic ones which packed a terrific punch, so it was worth listening to them carefully. Her students always came out top in French exams. For several years she had been a great friend of the Palmers. Jonathan and his wife both taught at the same school, where

Sam and Linnet were pupils, and Madame Bonamy often came to their house for meals or joined them on family excursions, before she went into hospital for the last time and died.

"Why do people have to get ill? Why do they have to lose their jobs?" Sam asked her now, in his dream.

But Madame Bonamy did not answer his question. She had something of her own to say.

"Ah Sam, why, why did you do it? Non, non, non, ce n'est pas gentil! That was a wrong thing to do, you know well. You must give it back. You should not have taken it."

"Give it *back*?" he said, appalled. "But—how can I? That family are on a Greek island—on Kerimos—six hours' journey from here. How can I possibly take it back? I don't know their name—I can't even post it to them. They probably didn't live on the island—they were on holiday too—"

"Sam, Sam, why did you take it?"

He tried to explain. "It was such a funny book—it was making them all laugh so much—I thought—I thought perhaps it might make Father laugh, if it was so funny. *You* ought to understand that," he told her.

"Ah I see." She reflected in silence for a moment. Then she told Sam, "Well, it is still possible for you to return it. That will mean going into the past."

"Into the past? How in the world can I do that?"

"You must go back precisely to the point at which you took the book. Not a moment sooner, not a moment later. Put the book down on the beach where you picked it up."

"How can I get there?"

"You go backwards," explained Madame Bonamy. "That is not difficult. Write with this diamond pencil on the looking-glass. Write very small. First, place the book under the glass—so."

15

Sam, who had got out of bed, took the diamond pencil from her and stood before the mirror on the dressing-table. Simon the cat, uncurling himself, yawning, stretching, followed Sam.

"What shall I write?"

"You must write in backwards writing, beginning at the bottom right-hand corner. Each word back to front. Each sentence back to front. You must write everything that you did, every single thing that you have done today, backwards, beginning at the last minute before you got into bed."

"I see." Sam thought for a minute, then lifted his hand towards the glass.

"Attendez un moment," said Madame Bonamy. "This is important. As soon as you have replaced the book on the beach, *come straight back*; it is possible to come back very fast, as if you were quickly rewinding a tape. Do not linger for a single instant."

"Why not?"

"To go back, just for an instant like that, does not part the strands of time," said Madame Bonamy. "But if you stayed even a few moments longer, you would begin making differences, having effects on future events. Also, you might get lost."

The very thought made him shiver.

Quickly he began to write on the glass.

"Let me think then . . . I brushed my teeth; I took off my clothes; I came upstairs; I said goodnight to Father; I took the clothes down to Ma; I looked at the book: I put my rucksack down on my bed; I fed Simon; I helped get the bags out of the taxi . . ."

Minute by minute he navigated back through the long day, and each minute in its turn was recorded in tiny, spidery silver writing from right to left across the face of the mirror. At last Sam came to the point of recording: "I stooped and picked up the book and the towel both together."

And *there he was,* back on the cool, sunny beach, clouds already beginning faintly to mist over the sun, stooping down with the glossy paperback in his hand.

He laid it neatly where it had been before and straightened, looking about him, with an immense lightening of the heart.

One thing at least had been put right; one thing need trouble him no longer.

But then, with a shock of utter dismay, he felt fat Simon rubbing possessively against his leg. Fat cat Simon, who had no right in the world to be there on a Greek beach on the island of Kerimos!

And next minute one of the quayside cats, a thin, raggedy black tom, howled out such a frightful piece of insulting cat-language from the concrete steps close by, where they were building a café, that fat Simon, insulted beyond bearing, shot after the black cat in a flash; there was a flurry, a scurry, black and tabby fur flew about, and both cats vanished, yowling and spitting, under a half-built boat.

"*Simon!* Come back here!" shouted Sam in horror, and darted up the steps after his cat. But, hunt though he might all over the quay, his cat was nowhere to be found. There were dozens and dozens of crannies and corners where the two cats might have retired to carry on their dispute: up alleyways, under stalls, under boats, in crowded little food shops, or under the tablecloths and benches of tavernas. Almost at once the search began to seem utterly hopeless.

And all the time he could hear the voice of Madame Bonamy saying, *come straight back.* He knew he should not be there, that Simon should not be there. He did not dare speak to anybody, ask if they had seen his cat. Was he already parting the strands of time, by searching and calling?

Oh, if only Madame Bonamy were there!

I mustn't stay here in Kerimos by myself, he thought wretchedly. But to leave Simon here—how could he do that? What could he do?

Then a hopeful idea slid into his mind. Wild maybe, but hopeful. If it were possible to go back earlier still—go back to a time *before* the Kerimos holiday—before Simon was lost—

But how to do that, without the diamond, without the mirror?

Standing in miserable indecision, looking across the brilliant blue water of the harbour at the white houses on the far side, Sam heard the echo of another voice, remembered from long ago.

"Your mind is a mirror; your mind is a mirror reflecting the world, showing you the image of the world around you, and all you have ever seen in it."

Who had said that?

Never mind who said it, *it was true*! My mind is a mirror, Sam thought; I can write on it. I have to remember all that has happened to me, from taking the book, back and back and farther back, like unwinding a tape . . .

And, thinking hard, thinking for his very life, he began to remember.

Minute by minute he travelled back, and as he grew more expert at remembering, the minutes zipped by faster and faster, while he guided himself through the past with the skill of a skater or a windsurfer, steering towards marker buoys, watching out for mileposts as they flashed up and past him. There was the time Linnet broke her leg; the time the chimney blew off in a gale; the time he lost his watch; the time they had the French boy, Pierre, to stay; the time Granny came for Christmas; the time he and Linnet had measles— stop! *That* had been when Dad gave him Simon as a kitten to

18

cheer up a miserable convalescence, when his ears ached and his glands were all swelled up, and Linnet went back to school and he was still stuck in bed.

Stop! he ordered the minutes, and they whirled to a flashing conclusion and left him in his own bed in his own room in Camden Town; and there was Father, as he used to be, undoing a square cat-basket with holes in the sides, to reveal a roly-poly grey-and-black-striped kitten, who displayed no sort of anxiety or homesickness, but leapt confidently straight on to Sam's bed, and burrowed and trod himself a comfortable nest under the feather quilt.

"Measles medicine," said Sam's father smiling, "to help you pass the time till you're allowed to read again."

"Oh, Dad!"

Being deprived of books had been the worst part of measles.

"It's so boring lying in bed doing nothing," Sam had complained, and Dad said—yes, yes, it was Dad who had said it—"Your mind is a mirror, reflecting the world. Look into your mind and you can find any image that it has ever held. You can always find something there to think about, to entertain yourself."

Dad had said it.

"Can I come up?" called a familiar voice from downstairs. "Est-ce qu'on peut entrer?" and Madame Bonamy came into the bedroom carrying a pile of books. "Yes, yes, I know that you are not permitted to read, Sam, but I have come to read *to* you, so pay attention. Mary gives permission for this visit. Allo, Jonathan, mon vieux, have you heard the story about the horseman and the oysters?"

And in no time she and Sam's father were swapping lunatic tales and laughing their heads off, and Sam showed Madame Bonamy his new kitten burrowed under the quilt, and Ma had come up with a pot of tea and cups and a big mug of orange juice for Sam; it had been a memorably happy afternoon.

"Madame Bonamy," said Sam swiftly when there was a break in the talk, "I have to ask you something. I'm all tangled up in time, things just can't be worse or more complicated. Simon is going to be lost on Kerimos—how will I ever get him back?"

He would have liked to ask about Father too—how to unlock him, how to get him out of the marble prison—but how could that be done with Dad right in the room there, and Ma pouring tea? As it was, Sam's parents gave him puzzled looks, and Ma said, "Are you running a temperature again, Sam? Going to be lost on Kerimos, whatever are you talking about?"

But Madame Bonamy appeared to understand Sam and she answered, "Cats are not subject to time quite as humans are, Sam, perhaps you need not despair. Also there is a lucky charm with cats that I have sometimes used. When you walk up the hill on your way to school, count the cats in the front gardens as you go by—"

"Oh yes, I've often done that! If you get as far as nine, it's a lucky day."

"So; no need to instruct you, I see," she said, smiling. "You have discovered for yourself how to undo the time-chain."

Then she read aloud a French play to Sam, and his parents, though protesting that they ought to be correcting books, had stayed and taken parts; everyone had laughed at their bad pronunciation, and Madame Bonamy carefully tore a slip of paper from her notebook and inscribed a Z on it. "For the worst French accent in the country," she said, giving it to Jonathan Palmer. "Well," he objected, "I teach Physics, not French, what do you expect?" But Madame Bonamy said she knew the rudiments of Physics as well as French; one ought to extend the range of one's knowledge as wide as possible, she said. "It is never too late to learn."

Then she had left, calling from the stairs that she would let herself out and hoped to see Sam in class again next week. Sam wondered at the time why his mother gave Madame Bonamy such a loving, intent look, full of admiration yet sorrowful too, like that of an older sister who knows the troubles the younger one will have to meet. Later, Sam thought he understood that look.

Was that the last time Madame Bonamy had come to the house? It had been a long, long time ago.

Thinking these thoughts, Sam became aware that he was sitting up in bed, that he was awake, at home in Camden Town, and that the night was nearly over, the grey light of dawn came filtering in at the windows.

Good heavens. Had he dreamed the whole thing? Madame Bonamy, and her advice, and the journey back in time to Kerimos, the journey even farther back in time, to this very room?

Which layer of time was he occupying now?

Rather tremulous, feeling hollow and strange, as if his legs had been walking hundreds of miles while he was asleep, Sam got out of bed and tiptoed across to the dressing-table, to the mirror. Nothing was written on its surface: no faint, spidery silvery backwards handwriting—there was nothing to be seen but his own anxious face, pale and smudge-eyed, staring back at him from the glass.

But the book that had lain under the mirror was gone.

And, search as he might through his scattered belongings and all over the room, Sam could not find it.

Fat cat Simon was gone too. Which was worrying: dreadfully worrying. True, the window was open, and Simon often did go out, via the branches of a plum tree, towards the end of the night, on his own concerns; but how to be sure of that? Suppose he was still left behind, fighting the wild black cat on Kerimos?

But—wait a minute, wait a minute—what had Madame Bonamy said about that? About cats—?

Hastily, but trying to be as quiet as a ghost because it was still very, very early—yesterday at this time he would have been listening to the crowing of Greek roosters—no town traffic was abroad yet, no trains passing, no milkbottles clattering—Sam scrambled into his clothes and stole downstairs. He simply had to be sure about Simon, he could not bear another minute's uncertainty.

On his way to the front door he stopped, with a gulp that seemed to shift his heart on its foundations, at the sight of his father, Jonathan, still sitting, wide awake, silent and staring, in the front room, as he might have sat all night long.

"Oh—hallo, Dad," Sam gasped in a whisper—but trying to make his voice sound as ordinary as possible. "I—I got up early. I'm just—just going out to look for Simon."

His father's eyes moved in their sockets and regarded Sam; they held a vaguely puzzled expression.

"Dad," burst out Sam irrepressibly, "Do you remember once saying that your mind is a mirror? That you can look into it and see anything in the world, anything in the past? Do you remember that?"

Jonathan's eyes seemed to become even more puzzled; then there emerged a soft sound from him as if he were trying out his throat, preparing to speak.

"Do you remember, Dad," Sam went on in a rush, "do you remember an afternoon when Madame Bonamy came and read a French play to me, and gave you a Z mark for your bad pronunciation? It was the day you brought me Simon."

Slowly, as if movements were not something he was used to,

Jonathan pulled out a wallet from his breast pocket and began awkwardly and hesitantly thumbing through its contents. At last, from the very back, he pulled out a grimy slip of paper, on which was inscribed in ink a large flourishing capital Z.

He held out the paper; the eyes of father and son met over it, and both smiled, just a little.

Then Jonathan spoke in a rusty whisper.

"Where—er—where did you say that you were going?"

"Out to look for Simon. He's missing. I shan't be gone long, I hope," Sam asserted stoutly, trying to sound confident and cheerful. "When I come back I'll put on the kettle for a cup of tea."

And he walked out into the cool grey city dawn. Far off he could hear the voice of industry beginning to stir and rumble. But here, in this elderly residential neighbourhood, all was quiet.

Cats were out in gardens though; Sam saw the marmalade tom across the street, and the slinky grey from next door and the dirty black-and-white in the garden two houses along.

He moved on very slowly with his hands clenched in his pockets. It wouldn't do to go too fast, he wanted to give the cats time to come out into the front gardens. Let there be nine of them, he thought. And, Shall I ever find that book again? Or has it really vanished? Did I really see Madame Bonamy? Or was she just a dream? Can Mother and Father miss her as much as I do?

While he walked on up the hill—methodically noting the tortoiseshell at Number Nineteen and the Siamese at Number Twelve—two thoughts floated to the top of his mind and stayed there.

Perhaps Simon will be the ninth cat. And perhaps Father will have put on the kettle by the time I get back.

23

Wing Quack Flap

"It really *can't* be a healthy situation," repeated the Welfare Officer nervously. Her name was Miss Wenban; she was thin and pretty, with curly dark hair and a pink-and-white complexion. She came from the South and had not yet grown accustomed to tough Northern ways and the bleakness of Northern landscape.

"Healthy? Fadge! It's healthy enow!" snarled Grandfather.

Every utterance of Grandfather's came out as a snarl, partly because of the shape of his mouth, which was wide and thin like the slot in a money-box; it seemed meant for putting things in, not for words coming out. And indeed, while Grandfather ate his meals, grimly and speedily shovelling in hotpot, oatcakes, porridge or kippers, he always insisted on silence.

"Eat your vittles and shurrup, boy! Mealtimes is meant for eating, not for gabbing. Hold your tongue and gan on with your grub."

Pat, whose father had been Irish and talkative, could remember mealtimes at home in Manchester when the three of them, he and Da and Ma, had had so much to say to one another, arguing and joking and laughing, that the food had grown cold on their plates; and not because it was tasteless

24

food, either: Ma had been a prime cook. But that was long ago now.

Years ago it seemed, and was; three whole years.

Not that Aunt Lucy wasn't a good cook too. Ma's only sister: it would be funny if she weren't. Ma had been little and pretty and round, like a bird; Aunt Lucy wasn't very like her in other ways. But she really seemed to put her soul into her cooking, Pat thought; that, and trying to keep the cottage as tidy and clean as circumstances would allow. Aunt Lucy's soul didn't seem to come out in anything else she did: wan, silent and bedraggled, small and grey as the ghost of an otter, with bulging bloodshot scared eyes and flat, scraped-back hair, she crept about the house in a faded cotton overall and fabric slippers with the toes gone out of them. She winced nervously at Grandfather's thumps and shouts, although she had lived with them forty-eight years; and, as long as Grandfather was in the house, she spoke as seldom as possible.

Once, unexpectedly, she had said to Pat, "I can remember when cowslips grew on Kelloe Bank."

"And what if you can?" snarled Grandfather. "What's so remarkable about *that*? You going to sit down and write a letter to the *Northern Echo* about that?"

Aunt Lucy winced and trembled, sank her thin neck down between her shoulders, and went back to separating currants for lardy-cake. She had never been able to master reading and writing; it was a sensitive point with her, and Grandfather often referred to her disability, using it as a punishment, either for her or for Pat, whichever of them at that moment had exasperated him. If Pat had a bad report from school—which, luckily, was rare—or did something that annoyed Grandfather—which was much more likely to happen—Aunt Lucy was the one who always came in for the first blast of his ire.

"Hah! I can see you're going to grow up like your daft aunt there. No use to man or beast. Two of ye; what a prospect. Thank the Lord *I* shan't be around to have the job of looking after ye. Thank the Lord I'll be underground."

However it didn't seem probable that Grandfather would be underground for a long time yet; not long past his mid-sixties, he was hale and stringy as an old root. His coarse white hair stood up on end, thick as marsh grass; out of his red, wind-chapped face—which was only shaved twice a week, sprouted over with grizzled black-and-white stubble the rest of the time—glared two small angry pale-grey eyes, always on the look-out for trouble. Grandfather was in a rage about having been compulsorily retired from his job in the Council Roads Department; he was in a rage about the death of his daughter Sue, Pat's mother, and her husband Micky, in a flu epidemic; he was in a rage about the price of tobacco, and about Stockton United having been beaten by Middlesbrough; the only thing that did not put Grandfather in a rage, oddly enough, was the situation in which he, Aunt Lucy and young Pat were obliged to live.

This situation was why the Welfare Officer came calling so often. But Grandfather had taken up a rock-hard position about it, from which he would not be budged.

"No. No. *No!* I don't intend to leave this cottage. I was born here—and so was *my* granddad—and they're not getting me out of here till they carry me feet first. After that they can do as they damn well please—I don't care what they do with the place, they can blow it up if they like."

They would never do that, though. The little house itself was protected by all kinds of Acts of Parliament. It was listed and scheduled and selected for preservation because a building had always stood there on that site from way back, mentioned in Domesday Book if not earlier, and also because it was one of the very earliest examples of a weaver's cottage, and still had the loom, on which Grandfather's Granda had woven, in the back room. A great nuisance the loom was; Pat often longed to take a hatchet to it. Then he could have had a room of his own, instead of being obliged to sleep on the settee in the front room. Also the back room would have been less noisy, though damper than the front, being built into the side of the hill.

It was the location of the house, Kelloe Bank Cottage it was called, that caused Welfare Visitors to write pages of notes and Medical Officers to make continual reports to Health Committees.

Kelloe Bank Cottage stood, as its name suggested, halfway up a steep, almost vertical bank, directly between the concrete legs that carried one monstrous motorway, and looking down at another, which circled the foot of the bank, so that all day, and all night too, a thundering, grinding, roaring, oil-exuding, dust-hurling torrent of cars, trucks, tankers, and vans poured to and fro, to and fro, above and below.

The Welfare Visitors and Health Officers often found it difficult to hear or to make themselves heard above the din of the traffic; they tended to stagger away after their visits, shaking with strain and gulping down headache pills; but Grandfather and Aunt Lucy seemed to have developed an ability to hear normal sounds above the roar of motors, and so, after a year or two, did Pat; but then he began to suffer from a lot of bad sore throats and coughs.

That was why Miss Wenban was here again. Once more she had braved the approach to the cottage, which was not an easy one. You had to leave your car in the lay-by on the south side of the east-west motorway down below, climb over a stile, scramble down the embankment, and then trudge

27

along a nasty squelchy footpath which ran through a tunnel under the motorway; emerging on the northern side, you scrabbled your way up an even steeper track to the cottage, whose tidily kept garden, with rows of leeks and cabbages, hung down before it like a striped apron spread over the hillside. Another path led round the cottage and upward from the rear, right under the massive legs of the north-south motorway, and so on up Kelloe Bank; but you could not get very far that way, for the top of the ridge was ruled across, like the seam on a football, by a tremendous barbed-wire fence and a row of mighty pylons guarded with DANGER signs; beyond that, the other side of the hill was the property of Kelloe Bank Generating Station, and eight huge cooling-towers stood in a group like giants' pepper-pots blocking the access to the plain.

Aunt Lucy believed the cooling towers leaked electricity.

"You can feel it in the air, often; and you can hear it ticking," she whispered confidentially to Miss Wenban. Grandfather, in a rage with what he called 'women's clack', had gone out, muttering venomous things under his breath, and was hoeing between the rows of vegetables, or Lucy would never have found the courage to speak.

With her trembling little claw she took hold of Miss Wenban's arm.

"Sometimes you can hear the air tick, like the sound of a spider making its web; other times it's more like a lark singing, or the hum of a bee. When it ticks, I'm scared to strike a match, in case the spark sets off the whole house."

"It's the exhaust fumes that bother *me*," said Miss Wenban, looking at Aunt Lucy rather hopelessly. Then she nibbled the delicious crumbly, buttery wedge of parkin, and sipped the hot fresh cup of tea that Aunt Lucy had set by her on a small tin tray painted with lilies of the valley. "I worry about all the carbon monoxide that must be pouring into your lungs—this is no place for you to live."

"Dad won't ever, ever shift from this cottage," whispered Aunt Lucy, "And I don't see how we could manage without him. He does all the shopping, you see, in Coalshiels; I never go out any more; I haven't left the house in twenty years."

"Why not?"

"Dad thinks better not. I might get lost. It's all so different now from when I was a girl."

"I could take you about, Auntie," offered Pat. "Or I could do the shopping, on my way home from school."

The yellow school bus stopped for Pat every morning, pulling into the lay-by, and brought him back at teatime; on the days when he was well enough to go to school.

"Four and a half weeks you've missed this term, Pat," said Miss Wenban. "That's awful, you know, in a nine-week term; it's half your education gone."

"I'm sorry," croaked Pat, and he was. "It isn't that I don't like school. And I read when I'm at home, books from the school library. It's my bad throats."

"Is it bad now? Open your mouth. Yes, I can see it is."

Miss Wenban was bothered, also, by the fact that Pat could not bring friends home.

"I have friends at school, all right," he assured her. "But their parents won't let them come here. Too dangerous. It'd mean biking along the motorway."

"Nowt to stop 'em coming over the watermeadows, the way I go to get the vittles," growled Grandfather, who had been driven back indoors by a heavy shower. You couldn't hear the rain because of the traffic roar, but you could see rivulets of water making clean lines on the exhaust-grimed

29

windows. "Mind, I'm not complaining," Grandfather added. "Who wants a passel of young 'uns about the place? Not I. *One*'s bad enow." He directed a scowl at Pat, which made Miss Wenban say firmly,

"Pat ought to have company. It's not good for a lad always to be with his elders."

Specially when one of them's a bit simple, Pat could see her thinking, though she was too tactful to say it.

In Pat's view, Aunt Lucy was not daft. Just scared off balance by Grandfather, was the conclusion he had come to; otherwise she was sensible enough, when you got her on her own. If it weren't for the horribleness of Da and Ma dying, Pat often thought it was a lucky thing for Aunt Lucy that he had come to live at Kelloe Bank Cottage; since his arrival she had brightened up a bit, and they had tiny secrets together when Grandfather was out of the way, over swallows' nests and butterflies, and things Pat told her about school.

"I suppose you can't have radio or TV here under the viaduct—" went on Miss Wenban.

"Who wants that trash? Pack o' rubbish!" snorted Grandfather.

"But if Pat could keep a pet, now? A—a kitten, or a budgerigar?"

"And isn't *that* just like women's fimble-famble?" burst out Grandfather with utter scorn. "Why would giving the boy a *kitten* cure his sore throat? Any road, I won't have a bird twitterin' and messin' about the house. That I tell you straight! Nor a cat, either."

Pat said nothing. He had once *had* a kitten, a little black-and-white cat named Whisky, brought with him when he came to Kelloe Bank Cottage from Manchester. Grandfather had thrown Whisky out one rainy night, in order to punish Pat for what he called 'sulks and whinges'; Pat still held his

30

mind well away from the memory of Whisky's end, flattened under the wheels of a petrol-tanker.

"Just the same, you should have something. What kind of a pet could you keep here? Perhaps a goldfish?"

Miss Wenban was not going to let Grandfather put her down.

"I don't think I'd want a goldfish, thank you," croaked Pat politely.

"Oh. Um." Miss Wenban was momentarily at a standstill. "Well, I shall think about it and come up with some other suggestions next week," and she left before Grandfather could sneer or snarl any more, edging her way through heavy rain down the steep track. Pat watched her with concern through the rain-washed window; he liked Miss Wenban and understood that she meant kindly by him and Aunt Lucy, though her visits tended to bring them much more trouble than if she had stayed away.

"Nearly went tail over tip *that* time," commented Grandfather, watching with a sour grin as the Welfare Visitor slid and just managed to recover her balance. "It'd be a right laugh if she slipped down the bank and went under a truck. Mayhap then the rest of 'em wouldn't be so keen to come pestering us, nosy-parkering in what's none o' their ruddy business. And as for *you—you* just lick her boots!" he grated out, rounding on Lucy. "Wha' d'you want to go feeding her tea an' parkin for? Who told you to do that?"

Poor Lucy started with terror and dropped a plate on the stone floor. Luckily it was only an enamel plate, but a chip flew off and Grandfather stormed at her.

"Now look what you've done! Blubberfingers!"

Fortunately at that moment he noticed that the rain had eased off, and so he went out to resume his garden work.

Lucy rubbed her thumb over the chipped enamel, sucked

in her breath, and gave Pat a nervous fluttering smile. She had gone red and white in patches, all over her face, as she mostly did when Grandfather shouted at her.

"Never mind, Aunt Lucy," Pat comforted her. "April's nearly here. Soon Grandfather will be out of doors most of the day. And your chilblains will get better. And my sore throats usually stop in April. Let's have a nibble of parkin," he went on, trying to cheer her, though he found it hard to swallow. "It's grand—the best you ever made."

But Aunt Lucy was struggling to say something.

"A pet—Miss Wenban—she says you ought to have a pet—"

"Nah," Pat told her quickly. "I don't *want* a pet. It—it just wouldn't do here—not with Grandfather and all . . ."

Aunt Lucy nodded a great many times, very rapidly, with fluttering eyelids.

"When I was a gal—had a collie dog—Lassie—" she whispered presently. "Your Uncle Frank—got her for me—time he want to sea."

Pat nodded. Letters from Uncle Frank arrived from places like Hong Kong and Sydney and Recife and Bombay; Uncle Frank, in the Merchant Navy, was a great traveller. And sounded a kind man.

"Your Granda—never did like Lassie," Aunt Lucy whispered. "Didn't like her at all." Pat nodded again. He could easily guess the kind of thing that had happened to Lassie. He put an arm round Aunt Lucy and hugged her.

"Never mind, Auntie! Who wants an old pet that's always needing its water changed, or its sand-tray emptied?"

Then Aunt Lucy surprised him.

"Got a pet! You—you can share her."

"*You've* got a pet, Aunt Lucy?"

Pat stared around the familiar little front room in

bewilderment. Was Aunt Lucy really a bit daft, a bit touched in her wits? He studied the grimy windows, the lace curtains that Aunt Lucy did her best to keep clean, the grubby red inner curtains, the shabby settee, the table with red chenille cloth matching the curtains, three wooden chairs, dresser with plates and pots, mantelshelf with clock and matches, fireplace with built-in oven; on the walls, two pictures of the sea and a calendar with a windmill; on the high shelf a lustre cup (*A Present from Scarborough*) and a Chinese teapot, a present from Uncle Frank. Twice he let his eyes roam all round the room. Upstairs, Aunt Lucy's room contained no more than bed, chair, clothes-hook on the back of the door, and window. Well, he decided, it's just a bit of her fancy, like the electricity leaking from the cooling-towers. I won't fuss her about it.

Aloud, he said, "Can I have a bit more hot in this cup, Aunt Lucy? I let it get cold while Miss Wenban was here."

She poured him half a cupful from the old brown pot; it was still hot, and he drank it in slow, careful sips, letting it slide gently down his sore throat. Doing so, he allowed his eyes to slip out of focus, so that he was able to see two blue teacups and three brown segments of tea, two pointing to right and left, a joined one meeting in the middle of his nose.

"Chinese duck's my pet!" whispered Aunt Lucy, with a triumphant smile. Her face for a moment was quite bright and lively, reminded him of Ma. But don't think of Ma, don't, don't, don't. Aunt Lucy went on. "I keep her in Uncle Frank's teapot. Name's Wing Quack Flap." She nodded and smiled, and said again, "You can share her."

Pat nearly choked on his tea. Gulping down the last mouthful he set his cup carefully back on the saucer, while his eyes winked back into focus. But — astonishingly — just before they did so, he could have sworn that he saw a beautiful shining duck, a mandarin duck, fly across the room. The duck was transparent, ghostly, it was like the double images that he had seen when his eyes were out of focus. Through its colours he could see the brown pattern of the wallpaper behind. But the colours were brilliant—red, pink, snowy white, deep blue, dark lustrous green. The duck circled the room once at speed, then vanished inside Uncle Frank's Chinese teapot— which was far, far too small to contain the bird that had flown into it. There could not possibly have been enough room inside. Besides, the lid was on.

"I'm going barmy, too," Pat thought. "Head aches. Better take an aspirin."

"Wing Quack Flap," whispering Aunt Lucy again, with that quick, twitching smile, her bulgy eyes flitting towards the window, outside which Grandfather could be heard digging and grunting. Then she took the brown teapot to empty the swillings outside.

While she was out, Pat climbed on one of the chairs, lifted down the Chinese teapot, and looked inside. As he had expected, there was nothing. He carefully put it back, and then, somehow, he must have slipped, for the next thing he knew was that he was lying on the floor, and Aunt Lucy was clucking and exclaiming over him.

"I feel a bit queer, Aunt Lucy," he croaked . . .

The fact that Pat was tucked up on the sofa having flu made no difference at all to the habits of Grandfather, who stomped in and out as usual, gnashing and growling. But fortunately the weather had taken a turn for the better, and at this season Grandfather was a dedicated gardener; he was out of the house more than he was indoors, hoeing, trenching, sowing, transplanting and mulching all day, while the traffic boomed and howled and fumed above and below him.

34

Wing Quack Flap

Pat could have his flu in peace, with Aunt Lucy and Wing Quack Flap to keep him company.

Aunt Lucy brewed innumerable hot drinks, which were all that Pat could keep down; Wing Quack Flap soared and swooped overhead, keeping him endlessly amused with her effortless aerobatics. Ninety per cent of the time she was airborne; she hardly ever alighted. Sometimes she flew through into the back room, if the door was open, and perched on the loom. Just occasionally she would come to rest on the red chenille tablecloth. When she did come to a stop, what charmed Pat even more than her brilliant colours was her friendly good-humoured expression. She was a little like Ma—always looked as if she were just about to break into a laugh. Very different from Grandfather! Her rosy bill curved in a permanent smile, her orange webbed feet turned out at a carefree angle, her black eyes twinkled with humour and knowingness. She shone in the dark little house where, despite Aunt Lucy's best efforts, everything was worn, everything was grimy and shabby from the exhaust fumes and dust that poured round the windowframes and under the door and through the curtains. But Wing Quack Flap was not grimy: she was shiny and glossy like a new horse chestnut just popped from its rind.

For the first day or two she was silent; but as Pat's flu took hold of him she began to quack: at the start, a comfortable contented gobbling noise, of the kind that ducks make when they are dabbling with their bills through muddy, weedy water: griddle graddle, griddle graddle, griddle graddle. Then, by and by, as she flew, she brought out a loud joyful honking quack: WAAARK, wark-wark-wark-wark-wark. Pat could hear it easily above the sound of the traffic, and he thought it quite the nicest noise he had heard since the days when his father used to sing 'Peg in a Low-backed Car' and

35

other Irish songs. Often Pat fell asleep to the sound of Wing Quack Flap's conversation.

"But, Aunt Lucy—is it right to keep her in the teapot?" he muttered one day, between temperatures, when Grandfather was out doing the shopping at Coalshiels Co-op. "The pot's too small for her."

"Nowhere else to put her. Nowhere that's safe," said Aunt Lucy.

There came a day when Pat's flu rose up like a river in spate and nearly swamped him entirely; when light and dark fled past one another in a flickering, speeding race like the headlights of the traffic along the two motorways; when Pat's thumping heart and his drawing, dragging breath made such a deal of noise that he was unable to hear the trucks and tankers above and below; when Doctor Dilip Rao came from Coalshiels, and a nurse in dark blue and brass buttons from Hutton End; when there was talk about an ambulance and hospital; only, they were saying to each other, how could they manage to carry a stretcher up the steep slippery path, let alone through the narrow tunnel under the Hawtonstall Highway?

In the middle of their argument Pat sat up in bed, watching the zig-zags of Wing Quack Flap, who was in the back room playing follow-my-leader with herself in and out of great-great-grandfather's loom.

"I'd rather stay at home," he announced. "I'd rather stay with Aunt Lucy and Wing Quack Flap."

No one paid any heed to his actual words: they were all so startled to see him sit up and act like a human being.

"Peck o' silly chatteration, talk o' fetching the boy to hospital," growled Grandfather, stumping in out of the garden. "Nowt ails the lad but a touch o' grip; and that's on its way out. Young 'uns weren't mollycoddled in hospital when *I* were a lad; you stayed home an' got better by yoursen." He scowled at Doctor Dilip.

"Well—" said the doctor. "In view of the difficulty with the ambulance—" He glanced at Nurse Enderby.

"I'll come in again this afternoon," she promised. "And first thing tomorrow."

Aunt Lucy said nothing at all but looked nervously from one to the other. While the doctor examined Pat she had taken Nurse Enderby into the back room and held a conversation with her, pressed up against the loom. Now Lucy was kneading and wringing her hands as if she rolled a strip of lardy-cake dough on a floured board. And if anyone had stood close beside her, they might have heard her whisper, "It isn't right, it isn't right, it isn't right!"

Dr Dilip and Nurse Enderby left, and Pat let himself slip down under the covers again. He felt tired and giddy from so much company.

"I'll make that call for you," murmured the nurse to Aunt Lucy on her way out. Luckily Grandfather did not hear.

"Beef tea—put on a kettle—make a cup of hot—" fluttered Aunt Lucy, and took the brown jug from the dresser and went out to the tap at the side of the cottage.

"Now those daft poke-noses have left—" snarled Grandfather, suddenly rounding with unexpected savagery on Pat as he lay limp under the blanket of knitted squares "—now *they're* out of the road, what was that I heard you say about your Aunt Lucy and some rubbish?"

Pat felt weak and hopeless. He could not protect himself from Grandfather's little grey gimlet eyes, which bored into Pat like laser beams, and his grating, angry voice which demanded again:

"What was that I heard you say? Quack quack flip flap—or something daft?"

"Wing Quack Flap is *not* daft!" feverishly flung back Pat. "She's not daft—she's our duck, our beautiful duck—and she lives in the Chinese teapot—"

"*What* did you say? I'll give you Chinese teapot, my lad!" roared Grandfather. "I'm not having *you* grow up ninepence-in-the-shilling, like your sawney aunt! I'm stopping any such nonsense *now*—once and for all. Wing Quack Flap, indeed! I twisted *that* perishing bird's neck twenty years ago, and all! I'll have no more of it now!"

And he strode across to where he could reach the high shelf, stretched up, and seized hold of the Chinese teapot.

"Wait, you, till I get this window open—Wing Quack Flap, indeed!"

"Grandfather, *no!*" cried Pat in agony.

But Grandfather, with a great swing back of his arm, had hurled the teapot out through the open window—flung it so hard and savagely that Pat, waiting for the crash against the garden wall, heard, instead, a shriek of brakes down below on the motorway, and then the tinkle of smashed glass, and shouts, and horns blaring.

"What in the *world* is going on in here?" demanded Miss Wenban, the Welfare Visitor, walking into the room just at the moment.

Grandfather had been taken down to the police station to be charged. Not with manslaughter—mercifully for him—because in the pile-up caused when the teapot he had thrown out went through the windscreen of an articulated car-transporter, although numerous people were hurt, and thousands of pounds' worth of damage had been done, nobody had actually died. But when the police came up to the cottage, Grandfather had flown into such a passion and resisted arrest so ferociously that he was now in a cell and

38

would probably remain there for some days. But that was all right, for Uncle Frank was flying home from Naples, where Nurse Enderby had managed to contact him by radio telephone.

"He says he was thinking of retiring this year in any case," Nurse Enderby told Aunt Lucy and Pat. "Thank you, Miss Blackhall, I wouldn't say no to another cup of your tea, and a sliver of that lardy-cake. Your brother said he had it in mind to start a little baker's shop in Tunstall, and maybe you and the boy could live with him there."

"Then Granda can stay here on his own," said Pat, comfortably leaning back on his sagging heap of cushions. "He'll like that better than having us."

Aunt Lucy nodded several times without speaking. But her eyes shone brighter than they had for months.

After Nurse Enderby had gone, Pat said sadly, "I'm sorry, I'm very sorry about—about your teapot, Aunt Lucy. It was all my fault. I shouldn't have said anything to Grandfather. And I'm sorry about—"

The name stuck in his throat. Already he was beginning to wonder if Wing Quack Flap had existed at all, in any way—or had she simply been part of his illness? Had he made up the whole thing?

But Aunt Lucy, nodding over and over, wide-eyed, solemn, patted his hand several times and whispered, "Never mind, never mind! Can't be helped. Besides—you were right. Teapot not big enough. No! But listen now—listen!"

Shaking her head, muttering scoldingly to herself, she pattered away to the window and opened it wide. "Not too cold now. Listen!" she said again. "Listen, Pat!"

Outside, April twilight was thickening, and though the traffic roar could still be heard, at this time of the evening the noise had diminished a little; indeed, as Aunt Lucy stood by the casement, her finger conspiratorially to her lips, a brief lull came, in which no vehicle passed on either highway, above or below.

And during that lull something else could be heard instead: a loud series of triumphant honking quacks: WAAARK, WAAARK, WAAARK, wark-wark-wark-wark-wark. Round and round the house the cry circled, three, four, five, six times; then, fading away, it receded into the far distance.

Back to China, perhaps, thought Pat.

Soon the traffic roar began again.

Snow Horse

A pleasant place, the Forest Lodge Inn seemed, as you rode up the mountain track, with its big thatched barns and stables all around, the slate-paved courtyard in front, and the solidity of the stone house itself, promising comfort and good cheer. But, inside, there was a queer chill; guests could never get warm enough in bed, pile on howeversomany blankets they might; the wind whispered uneasily round the corners of the building, birds never nested in its eaves, and travellers who spent a night there somehow never cared to come back for another.

Summertime was different. People would come for the day then, for the pony-trekking; McGall, the innkeeper, kept thirty ponies, sturdy little mountain beasts, and parties would be going out every morning, all summer long, over the mountains, taking their lunch with them in knapsacks and returning at night tired and cheerful; then the Forest Lodge was lively enough. But in winter, after the first snow fell, scanty at first, barely covering the grass, then thicker and thicker till Glenmarrich Pass was blocked and for months no one could come up from the town below—ah, in winter the inn was cold, grim, and silent indeed. McGall tried many times to persuade the Tourist Board to instal a ski lift on Ben Marrich, but the Board were not interested in McGall's profits, they wanted to keep their tourists alive; they said there were too many cliffs and gullies on the mountain for safe skiing. So between November and March most of the ponies would go down to Loch Dune to graze in its watermeadows, where the sea winds kept the snow away; others drowsed and grew fat in the big thatched stables.

Who looked after them? Cal did, the boy who had been fished out of a snowdrift thirteen years before, a hungrily crying baby wrapped in a sheepskin jacket. Both his parents, poor young things, lay stiff and dead by him, and not a scrap of paper on them to show who they were. Nobody came forward to claim the baby, who, it turned out, was lame from frostbite; McGall's wife, a goodnatured woman, said she'd keep the child. But her own boy, Dirk, never took to the foundling, nor did his father. After Mrs McGall died of lung trouble, young Cal had a hard time of it. Still, by then he had proved his usefulness, did more than half the work in the stable and yard, and as he was never paid a penny, McGall found it handy to keep him on. He ate scraps, got bawled at, was cuffed about the head a dozen times a day, and took his comfort in loving the ponies, who, under his care, shone and throve like Derby winners.

Ride them? No, he was never allowed to do that.

"With your lame leg? Forget it," said McGall. "I'll not have my stock ruined by you fooling around on them. If I see you on the back of any of my string, I'll give you such a leathering that you won't be sitting down for a month."

Cal had a humble nature. He accepted that he was not good enough to ride the ponies. Never mind! They all loved the boy who tended them. Each would turn to nuzzle him, blowing sweet warm air through his thatch of straw-yellow hair, as he limped down the stable lines.

On a gusty day in November, a one-eyed traveller came riding a grey horse up Glenmarrich Pass.

42

Snow Horse

McGall and Dirk had gone down with the Landrover to Glen Dune to buy winter supplies, for the first snows were close ahead; by now the inn was shut up for the season, and Cal was the only soul there, apart from the beasts.

The traveller dismounted halfway up the track, and led his plodding grey the rest of the way; poor thing, you could see why, for it was dead lame and hobbled painfully, hanging its head as if in shame. A beautiful dark dapple-grey, it must have been a fine horse once but was now old, thin, sick and tired; looked as if it had been ridden a long, long way, maybe from the other side of the world. And the rider, leading it gently up the rocky path, eyed it with sorrow and regret, as if he knew only too well what its fate would soon be, and what had brought that fate about.

Arrived at the inn door the traveller knocked hard on the thick oak with the staff he carried: *rap, rap!* still holding his nag's reins looped over his elbow.

Cal opened the door: a small, thin, frightened boy.

"Mr McGall's not here, sir! He went down the mountain to buy winter stores. And he told me to let nobody in. The fires are all out. And there's no food cooked."

"It's not food I need," said the traveller. "All I want is a drink. But my horse is lame and sick; he needs rest and care. And I must buy another, or hire one, for I am riding on an urgent errand to a distant place, a long way off on the other side of the mountain."

Cal gazed at the man in doubt and fright. The stranger was tall, with a grey beard; he wore a blue riding cape and a broad-rimmed hat which was pulled down to conceal the missing eye with its shrunken eyelid; his face was rather stern.

"Sir," Cal said, "I would like to help you, but my master will beat me if I let anyone take a horse when he is not here."

43

"I can pay well," said the one-eyed man. "Just lead me to the stables."

Somehow, without at all meaning to, Cal found that he was leading the traveller round the corner to the stable yard, and the long, thick-roofed building where the ponies rested in warmth and comfort. The one-eyed man glanced swiftly along the row and picked out a grey mountain pony that was sturdy and trim, though nothing like so handsome as his own must once have been.

"This one will serve me," said he. "I will pay your master ten gold pieces for it." Which he counted out, from a goatskin pouch. Cal's eyes nearly started from his head; he had never seen gold money before. Each coin must be worth hundreds of pounds.

"Now fetch a bucket of warm mash for my poor beast," said the traveller.

Eagerly Cal lit a brazier, heated water, put bran into the mash, and some wine too, certain that his master would not grudge it to a customer who paid so well. The sick horse was too tired to take more than a few mouthfuls, though its master fed it and gentled it himself. Then Cal rubbed it down and buckled a warm blanket round its belly.

Watching with approval the stranger said, "I can see that you will take good care of my grey. And I am glad of that, for he has been my faithful friend for more years than you have hairs on your head. Look after him well! And if, by sad fortune, he should die, I wish you to bury him out on the mountain under a rowan tree. But first take three hairs from his mane. Two of them you will give to me, when we meet again; tie the third round your wrist for luck. If Grey does not die, I will come back for him."

"How will you know that he is alive, sir?"

The one-eyed man did not answer that question, but said,

44

"Here is another gold piece to pay for his board."

"It is too much, sir," objected Cal, trembling, for there was something about the stranger's voice that echoed through and through his head, like the boom of a waterfall.

"Too much? For my faithful companion?"

Cal flinched at his tone; but the man smiled.

"I can see that you are an honest boy. What is your name?"

"Cal, sir."

"Look after my horse kindly, Cal. Now I must be on my way, for time presses. But first bring me a drink of mead."

Cal ran into the house and came back with the inn's largest beaker, brimful of home-made mead which was powerful as the midsummer sun. The traveller, who had been murmuring words of parting to his horse, drank off the mead in one gulp, then kissed his steed on its soft grey nose.

"Farewell, old friend. We shall meet in another world, if not in this."

He flung a leg over the fresh pony, shook up the reins, and galloped swiftly away into the thick of a dark cloud that hung in the head of the pass.

His own horse lifted up its drooping head and let out one piercing cry of sorrow, which echoed far beyond the inn buildings.

McGall, driving back up the valley with a load of stores, heard the cry. "What the deuce was that?" he said. "I hope that lame layabout has not been up to mischief."

"Stealing a ride when he shouldn't?" suggested Dirk, as the Landrover bounced into the stable yard.

Of course McGall was angry, very angry indeed, when he found that a useful weight-carrying grey pony was gone from his stables, in exchange for a sad, sick beast with hardly more flesh on its bones than a skeleton.

Cal made haste to give him the eleven gold coins, and he

stared at them hard, bit them, tested them over a candle, and demanded a description of the stranger.

"A one-eyed fellow with a broad-brimmed hat and blue cape? Nobody from these parts. Didn't give his name? Probably an escaped convict. What sort of payment is *that*? I've never seen such coins. How dare you let that thief make off with one of my best hacks?"

Cal was rewarded by a stunning blow on each side of the head, and a shower of kicks.

"Now I have to go down into town again to show these coins to the bank, and it's all your fault, you little no-good. And I'm not giving stable-room and good fodder to that spavined cripple. It can go out in the bothy. And strip that blanket off it!"

The bothy was a miserable tumbledown shed, open on two sides to the weather. Cal dared not argue with his master—that would only have earned him another beating or a tooth knocked out—but he did his best to shelter the sick horse with bales of straw, and he strapped on it the tattered moth-eaten cover from his own bed. Forbidden to feed the beast, he took it his own meals, and he huddled beside it at night, to give it the warmth of his own body. But the grey would eat little, and drink only a few mouthfuls of water. And after three days it died, from grieving for its master, Cal thought, rather than sickness.

"Good riddance," said the innkeeper, who by that time had taken the gold pieces to the bank and been told that they were worth an amazing amount of money. He kicked the grey horse's carcass. "That's too skinny even to use for dogmeat. Bury it under the stable muck in the corner; it will do to fertilize the crops next summer."

"But," said Cal, "its owner told me, if it died, to bury it under a rowan tree."

46

"Get out of my sight! Bury it under a rowan—what next? Go and muck out the stables, before I give you a taste of my boot."

So the body of the grey horse was laid under a great pile of straw and stable-sweepings. But before this, Cal took three hairs from its mane. One he tied round his wrist, the other two he folded in a paper and kept always in his pocket.

A year went by, and the one-eyed traveller never returned to inquire after his horse.

He must have known that it died, thought Cal.

"I knew he'd never come back," said McGall. "Ten to one those coins were stolen. It's lucky I changed them right away."

When spring came, the heap of stable-sweepings was carted out and spread over the steep mountain pastures. There, at the bottom of the pile, lay the bones of the dead horse, and they had turned black and glistening as coal. Cal managed to smuggle them away, and he buried them, at night, under a rowan tree.

That autumn, snow fell early, with bitter, scouring winds, so that from September onward, no more travellers took the steep track up to the Forest Lodge.

McGall grew surlier than ever, thinking of the beasts to feed and no money coming in; he cursed Cal for the slightest fault and kept him hard at work leading the ponies round the yard to exercise them.

"Lead them, don't ride them!" shouted McGall. "Don't let me see you on the backs of any of those ponies, cripple! Why the deuce didn't you die in the blizzard with your wretched parents?"

Secretly, Cal did not see why his lame leg should prevent his being able to sit on a horse. Night after night he dreamed of riding the mounts that he tended with such care: the black, piebald, roan, bay, grey, chestnut; when they turned to greet him as he brought their feed, he would hug them and murmur, "Ah, you'd carry me, wouldn't you, if I was allowed?" In his dreams he was not lame. In his dreams a splendid horse, fiery, swift, obedient to his lightest touch, would carry him over the mountain to wherever he wanted to go.

When winter set in, only six ponies were left in the stable; the rest had been taken down to the lowland pasture. But now a series of accidents reduced these remaining: the black threw McGall when he was out searching for a lost sheep, and galloped into a gully and broke its neck; the chestnut escaped from Dirk as he was tightening its shoe in the smithy, and ran out on to the mountain and was seen no more; the roan and grey fell sick, and lay with heaving sides and closed eyes, refusing to eat, until they died. Cal grieved for them sadly.

And, day after day, snow fell, until a ten-foot drift lay piled against the yard gate. The inmates of Forest Lodge had little to do; Cal's care of the two remaining ponies took only an hour or two each day. Dirk sulked indoors by the fire; McGall, angry and silent, drank more and more mead. Quarrelsome with drink, he continually abused Cal.

"Find something useful to do! Shovel the snow out of the front yard; suppose a traveller came by, how could he find the door? Get outside, and don't let me see your face till suppertime."

Cal knew that no traveller would come, but he was glad to get outside, and took broom and shovel to the front yard. Here the wind, raking over the mountain, had turned the snow hard as marble. It was too hard to shift with a broom; Cal had to dig it away in blocks. These he piled up on the slope outside the yard, until he had an enormous rugged mound. At least a way was cut to the front door—supposing that any foolhardy wayfarer should brave the hills in such weather.

Knowing that if he went back indoors McGall would only find some other pointless task, Cal used the blade of his shovel to carve the pile of frozen snow into the rough shape of a horse. Who should know better than he how a horse was shaped? He gave it a broad chest, small proud head pulled back alertly on the strong neck, and a well-muscled rump. The legs were a problem, for snow legs might not be strong enough to support the massive body he had made, so he left the horse rising out of a block of snow and carved the suggestion of four legs on each side of the block. And he made a snow saddle, but no bridle or stirrups.

"There now!" He patted his creation affectionately. "When we are all asleep, you can gallop off into the dark and find that one-eyed traveller, and tell him that I cared for his grey as well as I could, but I think his heart broke when his master left him."

The front door opened and Dirk put his head out.

"Come in, no-good!" he yelled, "and peel the spuds for supper!"

Then he saw the snow horse, and burst into a rude laugh.

"Mustn't ride the stock, so he makes himself a snow horsie. Bye, bye, baby boy, ride nice snow horsie then!" He walked round the statue and laughed even louder. "Why, it has *eight legs*! Who in the world ever heard of a horse with eight legs? Dad! Dad, come out here and see what Useless has been doing!"

McGall, half-tipsy, had roamed into the stables and was looking over the tack to see what needed mending. At Dirk's shout he blundered hastily out into the yard, knocking in his heedless hurry the lighted lantern he had set on a shelf.

He stared angrily at Cal's carved horse.

49

"Is that how you've been wasting your time? Get inside, fool, and make the meal!"

Then smoke began to drift round the corner, and a loud sound of crackling.

"Lord above, Dad, you've gone and set fire to the stable!" cried Dirk.

Aghast, they all raced round to the stable block, which was burning fiercely.

What water they had, in tubs or barrels, was frozen hard, there was no possible way to put out the blaze. Cal did manage to rescue the bay horse, but the piebald, which was old, had breathed too much smoke, and staggered and fell back into the fire; and the bay, terrified of the flames, snapped the halter with which it had been tethered in the cowshed, and ran away over the mountain and was lost.

The whole stable block was soon reduced to a black shell; if the wind had not blown the flames in the other direction, the inn would have burned too.

McGall, in rage and despair, turned on Cal.

"This is your fault, you little rat!"

"Why, master," said Cal, dumbfounded, "I wasn't even there!"

"You bring nothing but bad luck! First my wife died, now I haven't a horse left, and my stable's ashes. Get out! I never want to see your face again!"

"But—master—how *can* I go? It's nearly dark—it's starting to snow again—"

"Why should I care? You can't stay here. You made yourself a snow horse," said McGall, "you can ride away on that—ride it over a cliff, and that'll be good riddance."

He stamped off indoors. Dirk, pausing only to shout mockingly, "Ride the snow horsie, baby boy!" followed him, slamming and bolting the door behind him.

50

Cal turned away. What could he do? The wind was rising; long ribbons of snow came flying on its wings. The stable was burned; he could not shelter there. His heart was heavy at the thought of all the horses he had cared for, gone now. With slow steps he moved across the yard to the massive snow horse, and laid an arm over its freezing shoulder.

"You are the only one I have left now," he told it. And he took off his wrist the long hair from the mane of the traveller's grey, and tied the hair round the snow horse's neck. Then, piling himself slabs of snow for a mounting-block, since this was no pony but a full-sized horse, he clambered up on to its back.

Dusk had fallen; the inn building could no longer be seen. Indeed, he could hardly make out the white form under him. He could feel its utter cold, though, striking up all through his own body—and, with the cold, a feeling of tremendous power, like that of the wind itself. Then—after a moment—he could feel the snow horse begin to move and tingle with aliveness, with a cold wild thrilling life of its own. He could feel its eight legs begin to stamp and stretch and strike the ground.

Then they began to gallop.

When McGall rose next morning, sober and bloodshot-eyed and rather ashamed of himself, the very first thing he did was to open the front door.

More snow had fallen during the night; the path Cal had dug to the gate yesterday was filled in again, nine inches deep.

A line of footprints led through this new snow to the inn door—led right up to the door, as if somebody had walked to the doorstep and stood there without moving for a long time, thinking or listening.

"That's mighty queer," said McGall, scratching his head.

"Someone must have come to the door—but he never knocked, or we'd have heard him. He never came in. Where the devil did he go?"

For there was only *one* line of footprints. None led off again.

"He was a big fellow, too," said McGall. "That print is half as long again as my foot, Where did the fellow go? Where did he come from? I don't like it."

But how the visitor had come, how he had gone, remained a mystery. As for Cal, he was gone too, and the snow horse with him. Where it had stood there was only a rough bare patch, already covered by new snow.

Potter's Grey

They were hurrying through the cold, windy streets of Paris to the Louvre Museum—young Grig Rainborrow, and the au pair girl, Anna. They visited the Louvre two or three times every week. Grig would far rather have gone to one of the parks, or walked along by the river, but Anna had an arrangement to meet her boyfriend, Eugène, in the Louvre; so that was where they went.

Alongside one of the big main galleries, where hung huge pictures of battles and shipwrecks and coronations, there ran a linked series of much smaller rooms containing smaller pictures; here visitors seldom troubled to go; often the little, rather dark rooms would be empty and quiet for half-hours at a time. Anna and Eugène liked to sit side by side, holding hands, on a couple of stiff upright metal chairs, while Grig had leave to roam at will through the nest of little rooms; though Anna tended to get fidgety if he wandered too far away, and would call him back in a cross voice: "Grig! Grig, where are you? Where have you got to? Come back here now!" She worried about kidnappers, because of the importance of Grig's father, Sir Mark. Grig would then trail back reluctantly, and Eugène would grin at him, a wide, unkind grin, and say, "Venez vite, petit mouton!" Grig did not like being called a sheep, and he detested Eugène, who had large untrustworthy mocking black eyes, like olives; they were set so far apart in his face that they seemed able to see round the back of his head; and he had a wide, oddly shaped mouth, his curling lips were thick and strongly curved like the crusts of farmhouse bread, and his mouth was always twisting about, it never kept still. Grig had once made some drawings of Eugène's mouth, but they looked so nasty that he tore them up before Anna could see them; he thought they might make her angry.

"Hurry up!" said Anna, jerking at Grig's hand. "We're going to be late. Eugène will be waiting, he'll be annoyed." Grig did not see why it would hurt Eugène to wait a few minutes, he never seemed to have anything to do but meet Anna in the Louvre Museum. That was where they had met in the first place.

Standing waiting to cross the Rue de Rivoli at a traffic light, Grig was sorry that he lacked the courage to say, "Why do we have to meet hateful Eugène almost every day?"

But he knew that his courage was not up to that. Anna could be quite fierce. She had intense blue eyes the colour of marbles; they weren't very good for observing. Grig noticed a million more things than Anna did, he was always saying, "Look, Anna—" and she would say, "Oh, never mind that! Come along!" but the stare of her eyes was so piercing when she lost her temper, they were like two gimlets boring right through him, and she had such a way of hissing, "You *stupid* child!" making him feel pulpy, breathless, and flattened, that he did not say what he felt about Eugène. He kept quiet and waited for the lights to change, while French traffic poured furiously past in a torrent of steel, rubber and glass.

"Come on—there's a gap—we can go," said Anna, and jerked at Grig's hand again.

They hurled themselves out, in company with a French girl

who had a small child in a pushchair and, bounding on the end of his lead, a large Alsatian dog that she could only just control; as they crossed, the pushchair veered one way, the dog tugged the other, it seemed amazing that the trio had survived among the traffic up to this day. A tall thin white-haired man in pink-tinted glasses observed their plight, and turned to give the girl a helping hand with her wayward pushchair; a sharp gust of wind blew just at that moment, the dog tugged, the pushchair swerved crazily, and the pink-tinted glasses were jerked off the man's face to spin away into the middle of the road, just as a new wave of traffic surged forwards.

With a cry of anguish, the white-haired man tilted the pushchair on to the pavement, hurriedly passing its handle into the mother's grasp, and then turned back to retrieve his glasses. Too late—and a terrible mistake: a motorcyclist, twisting aside to avoid him, collided with a taxi, and a Citroën following too close behind the cycle struck the elderly man on the shoulder and flung him on to the sidewalk, where he lay on his face without moving.

If he had been wearing his glasses at that moment, they would have been smashed, Grig thought.

The mother with the pushchair let out a horrified wail: "Oh, oh, c'est le vieux Professeur Bercy!" and she ran to kneel by him, while, out in the road, all was confusion, with brakes squawking and horns braying, and a general tangle and snarl of traffic coming too suddenly to a stop.

Police, blowing their whistles, were on the spot in no time—there are always plenty of police near the Louvre.

"Come along, Grig!" snapped Anna. "We don't want to get mixed up in all this, your father wouldn't be a bit pleased—" For Sir Mark, Grig's father, was the British Ambassador in Paris. But it wasn't easy to get away; already the police were swarming round, asking everybody there if they had seen the accident.

"Oh, I do *hope* the poor man is not badly hurt!" cried the distraught young mother. "It is Professor Bercy, the physicist —I have often seen his face in the papers and on TV—it was so kind of him to take my baby carriage—oh it will be terrible if he is badly injured and all because he stopped to help me—"

A gendarme was talking to Anna, and, while she snappishly but accurately gave an account of what had happened, Grig slipped out into the street and picked up the professor's glasses, which he had noticed lying—astonishingly, quite unharmed—about six feet out from the edge of the road, among a glittering sprinkle of somebody's smashed windscreen.

"*Grig*! *Will* you come out of there!" yelled Anna, turning from the cop to see where he had got to, and she yanked his arm and hustled him away in the direction of the Louvre entrance, across the big quadrangle, before he could do anything about giving the pink-tinted glasses to one of the policemen.

"But I've got these—"

"Oh, who cares? The man's probably dead, he won't want them again. If he hears that you got mixed up in a street accident your father will be hopping mad. And Eugène will be upset—he'll be wondering where we've got to."

It seemed to Grig that the last of these three statements was the real reason why Anna didn't want to hang about on the scene of the accident. He pulled back from her grasp and twisted his head round to see if an ambulance had arrived yet; yes, there it went, shooting across the end of the square with flashing lights. So at least the poor man would soon be in hospital.

Well, it was true that if he was unconscious—and he had looked dreadfully limp—he wouldn't be needing his sunglasses right away.

Maybe he only wore them out of doors.

I'll ask Mother to see that he gets them, Grig decided. She'll be able to find out which hospital he was taken to, and make sure that the glasses are taken to him. Mother was fine at things like that, she always knew what must be done, and who was the best person to do it. She understood what was important. And—Grig thought—the glasses must be *very* important to Professor Bercy, or he would hardly have risked his life in the traffic to try and recover them. Could they be his only pair? Surely not. If he was such an important scientist, you'd think he'd have dozens of pairs.

The glasses were now in Grig's anorak pocket, safely cradled in his left hand; the right hand was still in the iron grip of Anna, who was hauling him along as if the Deluge had begun and they were the last two passengers for the Ark.

Eugène was there before them, waiting in the usual room; but, surprisingly, he didn't seem annoyed at their lateness, just listened to Anna's breathless explanation with his wide frog-smile, said it was quite a little excitement they'd had, and did the man bleed a lot? Then, even more surprisingly, he produced a small patissier's cardboard carton, tied with shiny paper string, and said to Grig,

"Here, mon mouton, this is for you. For your petit manger. A cake."

Grig generally brought an apple to the Louvre. Indeed he had one today, in his right-hand pocket. Eugène called the apple Grig's petit manger. While Anna and Eugène sat and talked, Grig was in the habit of eating his apple slowly and inconspicuously, as he walked about looking at the pictures.

"Go on," repeated Eugène. "The cake's for you."

Grig did not want to appear rude or doubtful or suspicious at this unexpected gift; but just the same he *was* suspicious. Eugène had never before showed any friendly feelings; the things he said to Grig were generally sharp or spiteful or teasing; why, today, should he have brought this piece of patisserie—rather expensive it looked, too, done up so carefully with a gold name on the side of the box? Eugène was always shabby, in worn jeans and a rubbed black leather jacket, and his sneakers looked as if they let in the water; why should he suddenly bring out such an offering?

"Say thank you!" snapped Anna. "It's very kind of Eugène to have brought you a cake!"

"Thank you," said Grig. He added doubtfully, "But I don't think people are allowed to eat in here."

"Oh, don't be silly. Who's going to see? Anyway, you always eat your apple—here, I'll undo the string."

It was tied in a hopelessly tight, hard knot—Anna nibbled through it with her strong white teeth, and Eugène made some low-voiced remark in French too quick for Grig to catch, which made her flush and laugh, though she looked rather cross. Once the string was undone, the little waxed box opened out like a lily to disclose a gooey glistening brown cake in a fluted paper cup.

"Aren't you lucky; it's a rum baba," said Anna.

As it happened, a rum baba was Grig's least favourite kind of cake: too syrupy, too squashy, too scented. He wasn't greatly surprised, or disappointed; he would have expected Eugène to have a nasty taste in cakes, or anything else. He thanked Eugène again with great politeness, then strolled away from the pair at a slow, casual pace, looking at the pictures on the walls as he went.

"Eat that up fast, now, or it'll drip syrup all over everywhere," Anna called after him sharply; and then she began talking to Eugène, telling him some long story, gabbling it out, while he listened without seeming to take in much of what she said, his eyes roving after Grig, who wandered gently into the next room, and then into the one after that, wondering, as he went, if it would be possible to slip the pastry into a little bin without being noticed.

"Don't go too far now—" he could hear Anna's voice, fainter in the distance behind him.

As usual, there weren't any other people in the suite of small dark rooms. Grig supposed that the pictures here were not thought to be very important; though some of them were his particular favourites.

There was one of an astronomer with a globe; Grig always liked to look at that; and another of a woman making lace on a pillow; she wore a yellow dress, and had a contented, absorbed expression that reminded Grig of his mother while she was working on her embroidery. There was a picture that he liked of a bowl and a silver mug, with some apples; and another of a china jug with bunches of grapes and a cut-up pomegranate that he deeply admired; Grig intended to be a painter himself by and by; he always stood before this picture for a long, long time, wondering how many years it took to learn to paint grapes like that, so that you could actually see the bloom on them, and the shine on the pearl handle of the knife, and the glisten on the red seeds of the pomegranate. Then there was a picture of a boy about Grig's age, sitting at a desk, playing with a spinning top. The boy was really a bit old to be playing with a childish toy such as a top; you could see that he had just come across it, maybe among some forgotten things at the back of his desk, and had taken it out to give it a spin because he was bored and had nothing better to do just then; he was watching it thoughtfully, consideringly; in fact he had the same intent expression as that on the face of the woman working at the lace on her pillow. Perhaps, thought Grig, that boy grew up to be some kind of scientist or mathematician (he must have lived long ago, for his clothes were old fashioned, a satin jacket) and at the sight of the top spinning, some interesting idea about speed or circles or patterns or time had come into his head. The boy with the top was one of Grig's favourite pictures, and he always stood in front of it for quite a while.

Then he was about to move on to his very favourite of all, when his attention was caught by an old lady who had been walking through the rooms in the contrary direction. She paused beside Grig and glanced out through the window into the big central courtyard. What she saw there seemed to surprise her very much and arouse her disapproval too. She let out several exclamations—"Oh, la la! Tiens! Quel horreur!"—put on a pair of long-distance glasses to take a better look at what was going on outside, stared frowningly for a moment or two more, then muttered some grumbling comment to herself, in which Grig caught several references to Napoleon III; then, shaking her head in a condemning manner, she went stomping on her way. After waiting until she was out of sight, Grig put a knee on the leather window seat and hoisted himself up to look out, in order to see what was happening outside that aroused such feelings of outrage in the old girl.

What he saw in the quadrangle made him surprised that he had not noticed it as they made their way in; but he remembered that then he had been looking back for the ambulance, and worrying about Professor Bercy's glasses, that must have been why he did not take in the oddness of the scene.

A wooden palisade had been built around the central part of the quadrangle, and it seemed that digging was going on inside this fence, a big excavator with grabbing jaw could be seen swinging its head back and forth, dumping soil and rubble in a truck that stood by the paling.

Then, outside the barrier—and this was probably what had shocked the old lady—three full-sized chestnut trees lay, crated up, on huge towing trucks, the sort that usually carry heavy machinery or sardine-like batches of new cars. The trees all had their leaves on, and their roots too; the roots had been carefully bundled up in great cylindrical containers made from wooden slats—like flower tubs, only a million times bigger, Grig thought. It appeared that the trees had been dug up from the central area and were being taken away, perhaps to be replanted somewhere else, just like geraniums or begonias in the public gardens. What on earth could Napoleon III have to do with it? Grig wondered, thinking of the old lady. Had he planted the trees, perhaps? They looked as if they could easily be over a hundred years old. Napoleon III had done a lot to beautify Paris, Grig knew. Perhaps among the roots of the trees, now parcelled up like bean sprouts, there might be coins, francs and centimes from 1850, or medals or jewels, or all kinds of other relics. I'd love to have a closer look at them, thought Grig, and, his left hand happening to touch Professor Bercy's sunglasses in his anorak pocket, at the moment when this thought came to him, he absentmindedly pulled out the glasses and perched them on his nose.

They fitted him quite well. He could feel that the earpieces were made of some light, strong, springy material that clung, of its own accord, not uncomfortably, to the sides of his head. The lenses, squarish in shape, were very large; in fact they almost entirely covered his face, so that he could see nothing except through their slightly pinkish screen. For a moment they misted over, after he had put them on; then they began to clear, and he looked through them, out of the window and into the courtyard.

For years and years and years afterwards, Grig went over and over that scene in his memory, trying to recall every last detail of it. When he had grown up and become a painter, he painted it many times—the whole scene, or bits of it, small fragments, differing figures from it—over and over and over again. "Ah, that's a Rainborrow," people would say, walking into a gallery, from thirty, forty feet away, "you can always tell a Rainborrow."

What did he see? He would have found it almost impossible to give a description in words. "*Layers,*" he thought. "It's like seeing all the layers together. Different levels. People now—and people *then*. People when? People right back. How many thousands of years people must have been doing things on this bit of ground, so close to the River Seine. And, there they all are!"

As well as the people *then*, he could see the people *now*; several students, a boy riding a bicycle, a policeman, and the three great chestnut trees, tied on their trucks like invalids on stretchers. And, sure enough, in among the roots of the trees, Grig could catch a glimpse of all kinds of objects, knobby and dusty, solid and sparkling; perhaps that was what Professor Bercy had been coming to look at? The glasses must have had a fairly strong magnifying power, as well as this other mysterious ability they had to show the layers of time lying one behind another.

What else could they show?

Grig turned, carefully, for he felt a little dizzy, to look inwards at the room behind him. The first thing that caught his gaze, as he turned, was Eugène's gift, the rum baba, which he still clutched awkwardly in his right hand. Through Professor Bercy's pink-tinted glasses the cake looked even nastier than it had when seen by the naked eye. It was darker in colour—dark blood-brown, oozy and horrible; embedded in the middle of it he now saw two pills, one pink, one yellow. The pills hadn't been visible before, but through the pink lenses Grig could see them quite distinctly: sunk in the wet mass of dough they were becoming a bit mushy at the edges, beginning to wilt into the surrounding cake.

Why should Eugène want to give him cake with pills in it? What in the world was he up to? With a jerk of disgust, Grig dropped the little patisserie box on the floor. Nobody else was in the room. With his heel, he slid box and cake out of view under the window seat, then wiped his fingers—the syrup had already started to ooze through the carton—wiped his fingers vigorously, again and again, on a tissue. He glanced behind him to make sure that his action had not been seen by Anna or Eugène—but no, thank goodness, they were still safely out of sight, several rooms away.

Turning in the opposite direction, Grig walked quickly on into the next room, where his favourite picture of all hung.

This was a painting of a horse, by an artist called Potter. Grig always thought of it as Potter's Grey. The picture was not at all large: perhaps one foot by eighteen inches, if as much; and the horse was not particularly handsome, rather the contrary. It was a grey, with some blobby dark dappled spots. Grig could hardly have said why he liked it so much. He was sure that the painter must have been very fond of the horse. Perhaps it belonged to him. Perhaps he called it Grey, and always gave it an apple or a carrot before sitting down with his easel and his tubes or pots of paint. The picture was over three hundred years old; a label said that Potter had been a Dutchman who lived from 1625 to 1654. He was only twenty-nine when he died, not old. Mother, who knew all sorts of odd things, once told Grig that Potter died of tuberculosis; which could have been cured these days. Grig thought that very sad. If Potter had lived now, he could have painted many more pictures of horses, instead of having his life cut off in the middle.

Anyway, this Grey was as good a horse as you could wish to meet, and, on each visit to the Louvre, Grig always walked to where his portrait hung, on the left of the doorway, between door and window, and—after first checking to make certain no one else was in the room—stood staring until his whole mind was filled with pleasure, with the whole essence of the horse; then he would pull the apple out of his pocket, take a bite of it himself, hold the rest up on the palm of his hand as you should when feeding a horse, and say, "Have a bite, Grey."

He did so now. But this time, something happened that had never happened before.

Grey put a gentle, silvery muzzle with soft nostrils sprouting white hairs out of the picture *and took the apple from Grig's hand.*

Then he withdrew his head into the frame and ate the apple with evident satisfaction.

Grig gasped. He couldn't help it—he was so pleased that he felt warm tears spring into his eyes, Blinking them away, he looked rapidly round the small gallery—and saw, without any particular surprise, that every picture was alive, living its life in its own way as it must have done when the artist painted it: a fly was buzzing over the grapes that lay beside the china jug, some men were hauling down the sail of a ship, the woman, winding the bobbins of her lace-pillow, carefully finished off one and began another. Then she looked up and gave Grig an absent-minded smile.

There were other people in the room too, outside the pictures, walking about—people in all kinds of different clothes. Grig wished, from the bottom of his heart, that he could hear what they were saying, wished he could speak to them and ask questions—but Professor Bercy's glasses were only for seeing, they couldn't help him to hear. You'd want headphones too, Grig thought, straining his ears nonetheless to try and catch the swish of a dress, the crunch of Grey finishing the apple—but all he heard was the angry note of Anna's voice, "*Grig!* Where in the *world* have you *got* to?" and the clack of her wooden-soled shoes on the polished gallery floor as she came hurrying in search of him. Grig couldn't resist glancing back at Potter's horse—but the apple was all finished, not a sign of it remained—then he felt Anna's fingers close on his wrist like pincers, and she was hurrying him towards the exit, angrily gabbling into his ear. "What in heaven's name have you been *doing* with yourself all this time? Can't you see it's started to rain and we'll be late, we'll have to take a taxi—"

All this time she was hurrying Grig through one gallery after another, and Eugène was walking beside them, looking a little amused and calmly indifferent to Anna's scolding of her charge.

Grig himself was still dizzy, shaken, confused and distracted. Firstly, he would have liked to stop and stare with minute attention at each of the huge canvases they were now passing in the main galleries. Because—just *look* at what was happening in that coronation scene with Emperor Napoleon putting the crown on his queen's head, and the Pope behind him—and those people struggling to keep on the raft which was heaving about among huge waves, though some of them were dead, you could see—and the lady lying twiddling her fingers on a sofa—and the man on a horse—they were all alive; it was like looking through a series of windows at what was going on beyond the glass.

But also, Grig was absolutely horrified at what he saw when he looked across Anna at Eugène; the sight of Eugène's face was so extremely frightening that Grig's eyes instantly flicked away from it each time; but then he felt compelled to look back in order to convince himself of what he had seen.

All the *workings* were visible: inside the skull the brain, inside the brain, memory, feelings, hopes, and plans. The memories were all dreadful ones, the hopes and plans were all wicked. It was like, from the height of a satellite, watching a great storm rage across a whole continent; you could see the whirl of cloud, the flash of lightning, you could guess at uprooted trees, flooded rivers, and smashed buildings. You could see that Eugène planned to do an enormous amount of damage; and it was plain that, here and now, he hated Grig and had a plan about him; what kind of a plan Grig didn't exactly know, but little details of it that came to him in flashes made him shudder.

"Come on, hurry up," said Anna buttoning her raincoat, when they reached the entrance lobby. "Button your jacket, put your scarf round. Eugène's getting a taxi, and he'll drop us at the Embassy and go on—"

"*No!*" said Grig. He didn't intend going with Eugène in any taxi. And he knew well that Eugène had no plans at all to drop them at the Embassy.

"What do you mean, *no*?" said Anna furiously. "What in the world are you *talking* about? Don't act like a baby. You'll do as I say, or else—"

"*No*," repeated Grig doggedly, and yanked at the wrist which she still grasped in an unshakeable grip. He looked at Anna and saw that she was not wicked like Eugène, but stupid all through, solid like a block of marble or plaster. It would all useless to argue with her and say, "Eugène is bad. He has some awful plan. Why did he put pills in that cake?"

66

Grig was still terribly confused and distracted by the complicated sights, the layers and layers of different happenings that were taking place all around him. But at last he realized what he must do. With his free hand he pulled the pink-tinted glasses off his face, and said, "Please, Anna. Put these on for a moment. Look at Eugène, when he comes in—"

"Oh, don't be so *silly*! Why in the world should I? Where ever did you *get* those glasses?" She had forgotten all about the accident, and Professor Bercy. "What is this, anyway, some kind of silly joke?"

"Please put them on, Anna. If you don't—" What could he do, what could he possibly do? Then, with a gulp of relief, he remembered some practical advice that his mother had once given him. "It sounds babyish," she had said, "but if ever you are in a tight corner, *yell*. It attracts attention, people will come running, that will give you time to think; so never mind that you may feel a fool, just do it, just yell."

"If you don't put them on," said Grig, "I shall scream so loud that people will think I've gone mad. I mean it, Anna."

"I think you already *have* gone mad," she said, but she looked at him, saw that he did mean it, and put on the glasses. At that moment Eugène came back through the glass entrance door, his black leather jacket shiny with rain, and on his face a big false smile. Without the glasses, Grig could no longer see the evil workings of Eugène's brain—which was in every way a relief—but just the same, he knew exactly how false that smile was.

"Okay," said Eugène, "venez vite, tous les deux—" and then Anna, looking at him, started to scream. Her scream was far, far louder than any yell that Grig could have raised, he had no need even to open his mouth. The smile dropped from Eugène's face like paper off a wet window; he stared at Anna first with shock, then with rage. "*Come* on, girl, what *is* this?" he said, trying to grab her hand, but she twisted away from him, still shrieking like a machine that has blown off its safety-valve. "No—no—no—get away—get away—you're *horrible*—"

By this time, as Mother had prophesied, people were running towards them, people were staring and exclaiming and pushing close, trying to discover what was the matter with Anna. Now Eugène's nerve suddenly broke. He let out a couple of wicked, hissing swearwords, turned on his heel, was out of the glass doors, and vanished from view. At the same moment Anna, furiously dragging the tinted glasses from her face, flung them on the stone floor as if they were poisoned, trampled them into fragments, and burst into hysterical sobs.

"Would you please telephone my father?" Grig said to a uniformed woman who seemed like someone in a position of authority. "I think my gouvernante has been taken ill. My father is the British Ambassador," and he gave her the Embassy number.

So they went home in a taxi after all.

"Please can you take me to see Professor Bercy in hospital?" Grig asked his mother next day, when Anna was under sedatives and the care of a doctor, and a new au pair girl was being advertised for, and in the meantime Lady Julia Rainborrow was leaving her ambassadorial duties to take her son for an airing.

But she said, "Darling, no; I'm afraid I can't. It was on the news this morning. He died last night in hospital; he never recovered consciousness."

"Oh," said Grig. "Oh."

He had dreaded having to tell Professor Bercy that his glasses had been smashed; but this was far worse.

I wonder if they *were* his only pair? Grig thought, plodding along the street beside Lady Julia. Or if other people—the other scientists who worked with him—knew about them too?

"Where would you like to go?" Grig's mother asked him. "It's not a very nice day—I'm afraid it looks like rain again."

"Can we go to the Louvre?"

"Are you sure you want to go there?" she said doubtfully.

"Yes, I would like to," said Grig, and so they walked in the direction of the Louvre, finding it hard to talk to one another, Grig very unhappy about Professor Bercy, dead before he had finished his life-work—and what a work!—while Lady Julia worried about Grig. But what can you do? You can't look after somebody twenty-four hours a day. Ambassador's sons have to take their chance, like everybody else.

Going quickly through the suite of dark little galleries, Grig came to the picture of Potter's Grey. He stood and stared at the dappled horse, very lovingly, very intently, and thought: Yesterday I gave you an apple, and you put out your head and took it from my hand, and I stroked your nose. I shall come back tomorrow, and next week, and the week after, and that will never, never happen again. But it *did* happen, and I remember it.

Do you remember it, Grey?

He thought that the grey horse looked at him very kindly.

The Old Poet

I had to fly to England for college interviews, and was going to stay there at least a month. My mother said: "Very good, you can go to your great-grandfather's funeral and represent this bit of the family."

"His funeral? But he's still alive."

"But Posy writes (Posy! What a name!) that the doctors don't give him more than three weeks at the outside. Well, it will be a release for her; heaven knows she has nursed him devotedly. I hope she is well rewarded for her trouble."

"Is he rich?"

"There must be a steady income from all those Collected Poems and Selected Poems and revised Collected Poems—and the verse dramas, they do those on the radio, I believe—"

My great-grandfather, William Beaumaris, aged ninety-eight, had three times declined the honour of becoming Poet Laureate. Didn't fancy having to cough up poetry to order, he said. Sooner write advertising copy about women's underwear. Which he had done at one time, to support his Muse. Posy was his fourth wife.

I had never met my great-grandfather because we lived in Kenya. And also because my mother had had a mortal row with him over the way he treated *her* mother. "As an unpaid secretary. Women were only intended as *vessels*, according to him." But that was all over forty years ago, and I certainly had a curiosity to meet this grand, mysterious old man, who had been at Queen Victoria's funeral and sat on Gladstone's knee, had known George Bernard Shaw, and went on a trip to Finland with Bertrand Russell. And had written more sonnets than Shakespeare, more lyrics than Herrick, more long obscure dramatic poems than Browning. Most of these I had not read.

I did read the lyrics, on the plane going to Heathrow. They were very lyrical but quite dry—half Coke, half lemon.

> The love I chased has turned to laurel
> and now repels my rash embrace
> armoured in leather leaves, her branches
> tough, brittle, sharp, and lacking grace;
>
> come autumn, when the molten forest
> shrieks at the gale with which it strives
> she stands, smug, safe, and wholly proper
> as guardian of suburban drives.

I never got around to the sonnets and the verse dramas; or, at least, not then.

When they asked, after my college interviews, where they should send the news of acceptance or rejection, I gave great-grandpapa's address—that created a startled and respectful silence each time—then I caught a train to Scotland, which was where he now lived, though he was not of Scottish origin; our ancestors were a Norman hanger-on of William I, and a Welsh princess called Nesta.

I had tried to telephone Posy, but could not get through; and Mother's letter had not received an answer, or not before I left home, so I had no idea what to expect, or even if *I* was expected. The last part of the journey entailed a bus journey over quite a large piece of Scotland, and then I found myself on the wrong side of a loch.

"Mr Beaumaris's place?" someone said. "Over there," and jerked a thumb. Half a mile away, over the water, among a great wedge of forest, I could make out the shape of grey buildings.

By this time I was nearly out of cash. With my last five pound note I paid a local to take me across in his boat.

"Ye'll know Mr Beaumaris?" he said sceptically. "There's a wheen newspaper folk try to interview him, whiles." His tone suggested that they never succeeded.

"I'm his great-grandson."

"Ay, is that a fact?" His tone was no less sceptical than before.

When he dropped me on a small granite pier I had half a mind to ask him to ferry me back again; suppose I found myself marooned in this tree-darkened spot (for the forest came right down to the edge of the water)? Suppose great-grandpapa had died while I was making my way to him? But I hadn't enough money to pay for the return ride, so I thanked the boatman, hoisted my pack, and set off through trees to the dimly glimpsed mansion.

As I drew near I could hear the sound of a chain saw: a malevolent, high-pitched shriek. The sound was ominous in those terribly silent woods. The trees were enormous. Under them grew a little grass, thin and moss-infested, like the sparse dandruffy hairs on an old man's head. There was a kind of path, and then a smallish open space. Beyond it I could see a side of the house, with a terrace and a row of windows; opposite the house lay the shore of the loch, which curved round here in a small bay. On the rocky shoreline grew a huge tree: it spread out like a hand, not a single trunk but about six

72

of them, grey and smooth fingers reaching upwards. At the foot of this tree stood a tractor, and up in the boughs were a couple of men, swinging themselves about, agile as monkeys, lopping off smaller branches. I thought they were amazingly carefree considering how high up they were—at least forty feet above ground—until, coming closer, I saw they wore crash helmets and were secured with safety harness which they had made fast to the main boles.

I was so absorbed in watching their operation that I did not, until I was quite close to them, see. the man lying on the quilted lounger, observing the men with an expression of deep hostility.

"And who the devil are *you*?" he snarled at me.

There was no mistaking who *he* was. I had seen that gaunt old face, that thin-lipped mouth and cockatoo-crest of white hair on plenty of book jackets and colour supplement pages. He was wrapped in a tartan rug and leaned against a pile of pillows; but he did not, to my eye, look as if he were within three weeks of death; far from it.

"I'm your great-grandson," I said. "William Malkin."

"And who, pray, gave you leave to come here?"

"Mother did write—to Posy—"

"Posy!" he growled, without troubling to pursue my story further. "Look what she's seen fit to have done. Do you know where we *are*, here? This is one of the last stands of true Caledonian Forest—and *she* has to send for men in crash helmets to spay that ash tree—a rowan, mark you, a mountain ash, magic tree, Thor's own tree—they are lopping it, they are crippling it, they are whittling it down to little more than a stump. Not only that, but they intend to tether the boughs together in some damned spider-web of steel chains—garrrrhhh!"

His growl was ferocious.

73

I said, "Why are they doing that, great-grandfather?"

"Delilah!" he muttered. "How does she know my heart is not in that tree? Or perhaps she does!"

"Perhaps the tree needs the treatment?" I suggested doubtfully.

One of the workmen, passing by, agreed with me. "Ay," he said in a scolding tone, "ay, man, ye should not have allowed that tree to grow in that gait; ye should not have allowed it in the first place!"

"I did not happen to be *here* a hundred years ago, when that tree first sprouted!" my grandfather hurled after him. Then he muttered to himself, "I daresay that fellow thinks I was here then. But I'll put a curse on them, I'll put a curse on the lot of them, so I will!"

"Are you able to put curses on people, great-grandfather?"

It seemed not at all improbable; he looked as if he had plenty of that kind of power in him. When he turned his blazing eyes on me I took a step backwards.

"Have I the power to curse? Of course I have! Ninety-three years of poetry—doesn't that add up to power? What happens to a gas when you compress it? What do you get? An explosion. Cool down air until it turns liquid—you could boil a pint of it on a lump of ice."

"Have you cursed many people then?"

"I'll tell you three I did curse," he said venomously. "Arnwit, Thoroughgood, and Threlkeld. Withered them up like raffia."

"But why? Why did you? Because they were bad poets?"

James Arnwit, Jasper Thoroughgood and Morton Threlkeld had been the poets who accepted the Laureateship when Beaumaris refused it. Arnwit and Thoroughgood had died, respectively of a stroke and falling under a bus; Threlkeld was fast approaching his end from alcoholism.

"Bad poets," he muttered. "Of course they are bad poets. And to have *them*—each in turn—offered the job when *I* was passed over . . ."

"But—good heavens—I thought it was the other way round?"

That was the story which had been spread about. Now I learned that it was not so.

"But why? You are a much better poet," I said in true family fervour.

With low-voiced hissing fury he told me why he had been repeatedly snubbed by the government. It was because of something he had done at Queen Victoria's funeral—*what*, I could not quite gather; unfortunately the chain saw gave a particularly virulent screech just then. Perhaps he spat at the coffin? Shouted a rude word or threw an egg? He would have been about fifteen at the time, an age when good manners have flown away on the breeze. Anyway, whatever it was, his action had deprived him of the Laureateship. And he was still in a rage about it.

"I'll curse them, I'll keep cursing them," he mumbled. And seemed gathering himself up to do so, when, nervously looking away from him, I saw a stunningly pretty girl approaching. Surely this could not be Posy? She looked no more than seventeen, blonde, with perfect features and huge grey-green eyes.

"Now *don't* get angry, don't," she wheedled, dropping down on her knees by his chair, and placing a soothing hand over both of his as they knotted and unknotted themselves on the tartan blanket. "It wastes your time, it wastes your power. Who's this?" And she turned the great eyes on me, inquiring, wondering, just a little calculating.

"It's my great-grandson," growled the old boy. He had never questioned my credentials; but it is true that I do look very like my mother, and she like hers.

"I am Meridian Jones," the girl informed me as if the name ought to be familiar. Another poet? And she added proudly, "I am William's acolyte."

I knew he had always had some teenage admirer fluttering around him wherever he was; it was to them that the lyrics were addressed. My mother often said she wondered how Posy stood them around the place; but she added, "I suppose they make themselves useful carrying trays and doing the dusting." This one didn't look like the sort to do any dusting; but she had brought a mug of malted milk out on a silver tray. Beaumaris swigged it down while Meridian Jones watched him worshipfully. Then she ran her fingers through his thick white hair, and said,

"Now don't think ugly thoughts about the tree-men; don't! They have to do their job. Make up a poem, why don't you, and I'll write it down. Make up a nice poem to me." She pulled a notebook from her jeans' pocket.

"I've written too bloody many poems. Poetry sucks the life out of you. It's like a fungus. I'd sooner curse somebody," he said fretfully. His angry eyes flicked about the clearing, and came to rest on me. I felt like the young lady of Smyrna in Lear's limerick 'who seized on the cat and said, "Granny burn that!"' I had not the least wish to fall under a curse just before going up to university.

At this moment a woman came round the corner of the house who must, of course, be Posy. She was in her mid-thirties, plump and smiling, with a serene, lived-in face and kind brown eyes.

"I was wondering when you'd turn up," she said to me. "You are William Malkin, aren't you? Did you get into your university?"

"What university?" grumbled the old man. "Why do you

want to go to a university? *I* never went to university. Didn't
need to."

"I shan't know for a week or two," I told Posy.

"You'll stay here till then, of course. We'll be glad to have
you—shan't we, Meridian?"

The younger girl gave me an admiring look.

At that moment the men in the tree began their netting
operation, slinging a steel cable from bole to bole, fastening it
with huge screws which they plunged deep into the timber.
The old man winced as each screw went in.

"Murderers! Torturers! Tying up the tree in a bloody
spider-web."

"Darling Will, it has to be done. Or next winter the tree
will blow down. It is done for the tree's own good. That's a
sick tree you have there."

"What's the use of being protected if you're half-dead
already?" demanded Beaumaris.

Meridian looked my way again, giving me a very sweet and
slightly knowing smile, as if she enlisted me on the side of
youth against the silly older generation. I saw my great-
grandfather notice this, and he did not like it. I thought he did
not want his disciple making eyes at young men.

Now the workmen came down the tree, hitched their
tractor on to a truck which had already been filled with the
piled debris of cut-off branches, and drove briskly away over
the grass, touching their crash helmets respectfully to Posy
and my great-grandfather as they passed by.

Beaumaris was speaking as the tractor trundled off, but the
noise it made drowned his words. He pointed a finger at me in
a hortatory manner.

"Now come along, darling," said Posy. "Time for your
nap. And you'll have to take it inside, for there's going to be a
storm, had you noticed?"

It was true; black clouds were piling up across the sky. Here under the huge trees the sky was only to be seen at all in small patches, but the light was dying fast; although only mid-afternoon it seemed like late evening.

A low chatter of thunder could be heard from the foot of the loch.

"Once we get a storm here," Posy told me, "it goes round and round. Trapped by the mountains, don't you see; it can't escape. Come along, Will, my honey."

She helped the old man out of his lounger. Meridian Jones fluttered around, rather unhelpfully, getting in the way and making gestures which came to nothing. Posy was quite capable of helping her husband indoors by herself. At length Meridian followed with the tray and empty mug, leaving me to fold the chair and take it indoors with the rug and cushions.

In the house, the old man was muttering about spider-webs as Posy helped him on to a day-bed and made him comfortable in a small room off the huge main hall.

"There would be spider-webs in the glass of the windows; and webs across their eyes; and spider-cracks in the glaze of their mirrors."

I could hardly decide if this were a poem or a curse; but the girl Meridian was enthusiastically jotting it down in her notebook, so I assumed that it was a poem.

"You come in here!" the old man called to me through the open doorway. I walked in nervously, as Posy nodded me to obey.

"Here." He pulled a ring off his thin middle finger. It was an old-fashioned gold signet with a black stone, jet perhaps, and a crest which seemed to be a spider-web. "Too late to leave you anything in my will. If that's what you were hoping?" he added in a nasty tone.

"Of course I wasn't!"

78

"Don't interrupt. You can have this to remember me by."

I didn't think I'd have the least trouble remembering him. Nor did he, for he laughed in a private kind of way, and went on, "It's the best curse of all. Come along: put on the ring."

Under his brilliant eye, what could I do? I slid on the ring—my little finger was the only one it would fit.

"Now *you* have the power," my great-grandfather said. "And much good may it do you. And now leave me in peace."

I went out and closed the door. Posy showed me to a huge damp upstairs bedroom with its own mahogany loo in a powdering-closet. The windows looked out towards the patch of grass and the shoreline where the old man had been sitting. So we had a grandstand view of the pale-purple flash of lightning which, at that moment, came jagging down out of the sky and struck the six-pronged ash tree, winding among the trunks like a bunch of flames in the hand of Jupiter. The tree flamed like an Olympic torch.

"Oh dear! After all that trouble and money spent," said Posy placidly. "Now, of course, Will is bound to say that putting that steel cable on the tree attracted the lightning. And for all I know he may be right."

Or he could, I thought, say that he had cursed the cable and the gelded tree.

But William said nothing, for he died at the moment when the lightning hit the tree; or at least this was a likely guess, for he was found quietly dead and cold in his bed, a couple of hours later, when Posy took him a cup of tea.

So I went to the funeral. The rude epithet shouted after Queen Victoria must have been overlooked, at last, or put out of mind, for the ceremony took place in the Abbey, with full appropriate splendours, and William was given a place in Poets' Corner. And all the time the service went on, I looked up at the windows and wondered if I could see spider-web cracks in them.

I was given my place at Oxford, but have derived little benefit from it, for my great-grandfather's curse came into operation almost at once: I began writing poetry, and find I have no time left over for any other activity. Poetry, as he said, sucks the life out of you; it is like a parasitical growth.

And with it comes the power to curse; but I have not used that yet.

Lob's Girl

Some people choose their dogs, and some dogs choose their people. The Pengelly family had no say in the choosing of Lob; he came to them in the second way, and very decisively.

It began on the beach, the summer when Sandy was five, Don, her older brother, twelve, and the twins were three. Sandy was really Alexandra, because her grandmother had a beautiful picture of a queen in a diamond tiara and high collar of pearls. It hung by Granny Pearce's kitchen sink and was as familiar as the doormat. When Sandy was born everyone agreed that she was the living spit of the picture, and so she was called Alexandra and Sandy for short.

On this summer day she was lying peacefully reading a comic and not keeping an eye on the twins, who didn't need it because they were occupied in seeing which of them could wrap the most seaweed around the other one's legs. Father—Bert Pengelly—and Don were up on the Hard painting the bottom boards of the boat in which Father went fishing for pilchards. And Mother—Jean Pengelly—was getting ahead with making the Christmas puddings because she never felt easy in her mind if they weren't made and safely put away by the end of August. As usual, each member of the family was happily getting on with his or her own affairs. Little did they guess how soon this state of things would be

81

changed by the large new member who was going to erupt into their midst.

Sandy rolled onto her back to make sure that the twins were not climbing on slippery rocks or getting cut off by the tide. At the same moment a large body struck her forcibly in the midriff and she was covered by flying sand. Instinctively she shut her eyes and felt the sand being wiped off her face by something that seemed like a warm, rough, damp flannel. She opened her eyes and looked. It was a tongue. Its owner was a large and bouncy young Alsatian, or German shepherd, with topaz eyes, black-tipped pricked ears, a thick, soft coat, and a bushy black-tipped tail.

"*Lob!*" shouted a man further up the beach. "Lob, come here!"

But Lob, as if trying to atone for the surprise he had given her, went on licking the sand off Sandy's face, wagging his tail so hard that he kept on knocking up more clouds of sand. His owner, a grey-haired man with a limp, walked over as quickly as he could and seized him by the collar.

"I hope he didn't give you a fright?" the man said to Sandy. "He meant it in play—he's only young."

"Oh, no, I think he's *beautiful*," said Sandy. She picked up a bit of driftwood and threw it. Lob, whisking easily out of his master's grip, was after it like a sand-coloured bullet. He came back with the stick, beaming, and gave it to Sandy. At the same time he gave himself, though no one else was aware of this at the time. But with Sandy, too, it was love at first sight, and when, after a lot more stick-throwing, she and the twins joined Father and Don to go home for tea, they cast many a backward glance at Lob being led firmly away by his master.

"I wish we could play with him every day," Tess sighed.

"Why can't we?" said Tim.

Lob's Girl

Sandy explained: "Because Mr Dodsworth, who owns him, is from Liverpool, and he is only staying at the Fisherman's Arms till Saturday."

"Is Liverpool a long way off?"

"Right at the other end of England from Cornwall, I'm afraid."

It was a Cornish fishing village where the Pengelly family lived, with rocks and cliffs and a strip of beach and a little round harbour, and palm trees growing in the gardens of the little whitewashed stone houses. The village was approached by a narrow, steep, twisting hill-road, and guarded by a notice that said LOW GEAR FOR 1½ MILES, DANGEROUS TO CYCLISTS.

The Pengelly children went home to scones with Cornish cream and jam, thinking they had seen the last of Lob. But they were much mistaken. The whole family was playing cards by the fire in the front room after supper when there was a loud thump and a crash of china in the kitchen.

"My Christmas puddings!" exclaimed Jean, and ran out.

"Did you put TNT in them, then?" her husband said.

But it was Lob, who, finding the front door shut, had gone around the back and bounced in through the open kitchen window, where the puddings were cooling on the sill. Luckily, only the smallest was knocked down and broken.

Lob stood on his hind legs and plastered Sandy's face with licks. Then he did the same for the twins, who shrieked with joy.

"Where does this friend of yours come from?" inquired Mr Pengelly.

"He's staying at the Fisherman's Arms—I mean his owner is."

"Then he must go back there. Find a bit of string, Sandy, to tie to his collar."

"I wonder how he found his way here," Mrs Pengelly said, when the reluctant Lob had been led away whining and Sandy had explained about their afternoon's game on the beach. "Fisherman's Arms is right round the other side of the harbour."

Lob's owner scolded him and thanked Mr Pengelly for bringing him back. Jean Pengelly warned the children that they had better not encourage Lob any more if they met him on the beach, or it would only lead to more trouble. So they dutifully took no notice of him the next day, until he spoiled their good resolutions by dashing up to them with joyful barks, wagging his tail so hard that he winded Tess and knocked Tim's legs from under him.

They had a happy day, playing on the sand.

The next day was Saturday. Sandy had found out that Mr Dodsworth was to catch the half past nine train. She went out secretly, down to the station, nodded to Mr Hoskins, the stationmaster, who wouldn't dream of charging any local for a platform ticket, and climbed up on the footbridge that led over the tracks. She didn't want to be seen, but she did want to see. She saw Mr Dodsworth get on the train, acompanied by an unhappy-looking Lob with drooping ears and tail. Then she saw the train slide away out of sight around the next headland, with a melancholy wail that sounded like Lob's last goodbye.

Sandy wished she hadn't had the idea of coming to the station. She walked home miserably, with her shoulders hunched and her hands in her pockets. For the rest of the day she was so cross and unlike herself, that Tess and Tim were quite surprised, and her mother gave her a dose of senna.

A week passed. Then, one evening, Mrs Pengelly and the younger children were in the front room playing snakes and ladders. Mr Pengelly and Don had gone fishing on the evening tide. If your father is a fisherman, he will never be home at the same time from one week to the next.

Suddenly, history repeating itself, there was a crash from the kitchen. Jean Pengelly leaped up, crying, "My blackberry jam!" She and the children had spent the morning picking and the afternoon boiling fruit.

But Sandy was ahead of her mother. With flushed cheeks and eyes like stars she had darted into the kitchen, where she and Lob were hugging one another in a frenzy of joy. About a yard of his tongue was out, and he was licking every part of her that he could reach.

"Good heavens!" exclaimed Jean. "How in the world did *he* get here?"

"He must have walked," said Sandy. "Look at his feet."

They were worn, dusty and tarry. One had a cut on the pad.

"They ought to be bathed," said Jean Pengelly. "Sandy, run a bowl of warm water while I get the disinfectant."

"What'll we do about him, Mother?" said Sandy anxiously.

Mrs Pengelly looked at her daughter's pleading eyes and sighed.

"He must go back to his owner, of course," she said, making her voice firm. "Your dad can get the address from the Fisherman's tomorrow, and phone him. In the meantime he'd better have a long drink and a good meal."

Lob was very grateful for the drink and the meal, and made no objection to having his feet washed. Then he flopped down on the hearthrug and slept in front of the fire they had lit because it was a cold wet evening, with his head on Sandy's feet. He was a very tired dog. He had walked all the way from Liverpool to Cornwall, which is more than four hundred miles.

The next day Mr Pengelly phoned Lob's owner, and the

following morning Mr Dodsworth arrived off the night train, decidedly put out, to take his pet home. That parting was worse than the first. Lob whined, Don walked out of the house, the twins burst out crying, and Sandy crept up to her bedroom afterward and lay with her face pressed into the quilt, feeling as if she were bruised all over.

Jean Pengelly took them all into Plymouth to see the circus the next day and the twins cheered up a little, but even the hour's ride in the train each way and the Liberty horses and performing seals could not cure Sandy's sore heart.

She need not have bothered, though. In ten days' time Lob was back—limping this time, with a torn ear and a patch missing out of his furry coat, as if he had met and tangled with an enemy or two in the course of his four-hundred-mile walk.

Bert Pengelly rang up Liverpool again. Mr Dodsworth, when he answered, sounded weary. He said, "That dog has already cost me two days that I can't spare away from my work—plus endless time in police stations and drafting newspaper advertisements. I'm too old for these up and downs. I think we'd better face the fact, Mr Pengelly, that it's your family he wants to stay with—that is, if you want to have him."

Bert Pengelly gulped. He was not a rich man; and Lob was a pedigree dog. He said cautiously, "How much would you be asking for him?"

"Good heavens, man, I'm not suggesting I'd *sell* him to you. You must have him as a gift. Think of the train fares I'll be saving. You'll be doing me a good turn."

"Is he a big eater?" Bert asked doubtfully.

By this time the children, breathless in the background listening to one side of this conversation, had realized what was in the wind and were dancing up and down with their hands clasped beseechingly.

"Oh, not for his size," Lob's owner assured Bert. "Two or

three pounds of meat a day, and some vegetables and gravy and biscuits—he does very well on that."

Alexandra's father looked over the telephone at his daughter's swimming eyes and trembling lips. He reached a decision. "Well then, Mr Dodsworth," he said briskly, "we'll accept your offer and thank you very much. The children will be overjoyed, and you can be sure Lob has come to a good home. They'll look after him and see he gets enough exercise. But I can tell you," he ended firmly, "if he wants to settle in with us, he'll have to learn to eat a lot of fish."

So that was how Lob came to live with the Pengelly family. Everybody loved him and he loved them all. But there was never any question who came first with him. He was Sandy's dog. He slept by her bed and followed her everywhere he was allowed.

Nine years went by, and each summer Mr Dodsworth came back to stay at the Fisherman's Arms and call on his erstwhile dog. Lob always met him with recognition and dignified pleasure, accompanied him for a walk or two—but showed no signs of wishing to return to Liverpool. His place, he intimated, was definitely with the Pengellys.

In the course of nine years Lob changed less than Sandy. As she went into her teens he became a little slower, a little stiffer, there was a touch of grey on his nose, but he was still a handsome dog. He and Sandy still loved one another devotedly.

One evening in October, all the summer visitors had left and the little fishing town looked empty and secretive. It was a wet, windy dusk. When the children came home from school—even the twins were at the local comprehensive now, and Don was a fully-fledged fisherman—Jean Pengelly said, "Sandy, your Aunt Rebecca says she's lonely because Uncle Will Hoskins has gone out trawling, and she wants one of you to go and spend the evening with her. You go, dear; you can take your homework with you."

Sandy looked far from enthusiastic.

"Can I take Lob with me?"

"You know Aunt Becky doesn't really like dogs—oh, very well." Mrs Pengelly sighed. "I suppose she'll have to put up with him as well as you."

Reluctantly Sandy tidied herself, took her schoolbag, put on the damp raincoat she had just taken off, fastened Lob's lead to his collar, and set off to walk through the dusk to Aunt Becky's cottage, which was five minutes' climb up the steep hill.

The wind was howling through the shrouds of boats drawn up on the Hard.

"Put some cheerful music on, do," said Jean Pengelly to the nearest twin. "Anything to drown that wretched sound while I make your dad's supper." So Don, who had just come in, put on some rock music, loud. Which was why the Pengellys did not hear the lorry hurtle down the hill and crash against the post office wall a few minutes later.

Dr Travers was driving through Cornwall with his wife, taking a late holiday before patients began coming down with winter colds and flu. He saw the sign that said STEEP HILL. LOW GEAR FOR 1½ MILES. Dutifully he changed into second gear.

"We must be nearly there," said his wife, looking out of her window. "I noticed a sign on the coast road that said the Fisherman's Arms was two miles. What a narrow, dangerous hill! But the cottages are very pretty—oh, Frank, stop, *stop!* There's a child, I'm sure it's a child—by the wall over there!"

Dr Travers jammed on his brakes and brought the car to a stop. A little stream ran down by the road in a shallow stone culvert, and half in the water lay something that looked, in the dusk, like a pile of clothes—or was it the body of a child?

Mrs Travers was out of the car in a flash, but her husband was quicker.

"Don't touch her, Emily!" he said sharply. "She's been hit. Can't be more than a few minutes. Remember that lorry that overtook us half a mile back, speeding like the devil? Here, quick, go into that cottage and phone for an ambulance. The girl's in a bad way. I'll stay here and do what I can to stop the bleeding. Don't waste a minute."

Doctors are expert at stopping dangerous bleeding, for they know the right places to press. This Dr Travers was able to do, but he didn't dare do more; the girl was lying in a queerly crumpled heap, and he guessed she had a number of bones broken and that it would be highly dangerous to move her. He watched her with great concentration, wondering where the lorry had got to, and what other damage it had done.

Mrs Travers was very quick. She had seen plenty of accident cases and knew the importance of speed. The first cottage she tried had a phone; in four minutes she was back, and in six an ambulance was wailing down the hill.

Its attendants lifted the child on to a stretcher as carefully as if she were made of fine thistledown. The ambulance sped off to Plymouth—for the local cottage hospital did not take serious accident cases—and Dr Travers went down to the police station to report what he had done.

He found that the police already knew about the speeding lorry—which had suffered from loss of brakes and ended up with its radiator halfway through the post office wall. The driver was concussed and shocked, but the police thought he was the only person injured—until Dr Travers told his tale.

At half past nine that night, Aunt Rebecca Hoskins was sitting by her fire thinking aggrieved thoughts about the inconsiderateness of nieces who were asked to supper and never turned up, when she was startled by a neighbour, who burst in, exclaiming, "Have you heard about Sandy Pengelly, then, Mrs Hoskins? Terrible thing, poor little soul, and they don't know if she's likely to live. Police have got the lorry driver that hit her—ah, it didn't ought to be allowed, speeding through the place like that at umpty miles an hour, they ought to jail him for life—not that that'd be any comfort to poor Bert and Jean."

Horrified, Aunt Rebecca put on a coat and went down to her brother's house. She found the family with white shocked faces; Bert and Jean were about to drive off to the hospital where Sandy had been taken, and the twins were crying bitterly. Lob was nowhere to be seen. But Aunt Rebecca was not interested in dogs; she did not inquire about him.

"Thank the Lord you've come, Beck," said her brother. "Will you stay the night with Don and the twins? Don's out looking for Lob, and heaven knows when we'll be back; we may get a bed with Jean's mother in Plymouth."

"Oh, if only I'd never invited the poor child," wailed Mrs Hoskins. But Bert and Jean hardly heard her.

That night seemed to last forever. The twins cried themselves to sleep. Don came home very late and grim-faced. Bert and Jean sat in a waiting room of the Western Counties Hospital, but Sandy was unconscious, they were told, and she remained so. All that could be done for her was done. She was given transfusions to replace all the blood she had lost. The broken bones were set and put in slings and cradles.

"Is she a healthy girl? Has she a good constitution?" the emergency doctor asked.

"Aye, doctor, she is that," Bert said hoarsely. The lump in Jean's throat prevented her from answering; she merely nodded.

"Then she ought to have a chance. But I won't conceal from you that her condition is very serious, unless she shows signs of coming out from this coma."

But as hour succeeded hour, Sandy showed no signs of recovering consciousness. Her parents sat in the waiting room with haggard faces; sometimes one of them would go to telephone the family at home, or to try to get a little sleep at the home of Granny Pearce not far away.

At noon next day Dr and Mrs Travers went to the Pengelly cottage to inquire how Sandy was doing, but the report was gloomy: "Still in a very serious condition." The twins were miserably unhappy. They forgot that they had sometimes called their elder sister bossy, and only remembered how often she had shared her pocket money with them, how she read to them and took them for picnics and helped with their homework. Now there was no Sandy, no Mother and Dad, Don went around with a grey, shuttered face, and worse still, there was no Lob.

The Western Counties Hospital is a large one, with dozens of different departments and five or six connected buildings, each with three or four entrances. By that afternoon it became noticeable that a dog seemed to have taken up position outside the hospital, with the fixed intention of getting in. Patiently he would try first one entrance and then another, all the way around and then begin again. Sometimes he would get a little way inside, following a visitor, but animals were, of course, forbidden, and he was always kindly but firmly turned out again. Sometimes the porter at the main entrance gave him a pat or offered him a bit of sandwich—he looked so wet and beseeching and desperate. But he never ate the sandwich. No one seemed to own him or to know where he came from; Plymouth is a large city and he might have belonged to anybody.

A Goose on your Grave

At teatime Granny Pearce came through the pouring rain to bring a flask of hot tea with brandy in it to her daughter and son-in-law. Just as she reached the main entrance the porter was gently but forcibly shoving out a large, agitated, soaking-wet Alsatian dog.

"No, old fellow, you can *not* come in. Hospitals are for people, not for dogs."

"Why, bless me," exclaimed old Mrs Pearce. "That's Lob! Here, Lob, Lobby boy!"

Lob ran to her, whining. Mrs Pearce walked up to the desk.

"I'm sorry, madam, you can't bring that dog in here," the porter said.

Mrs Pearce was a very determined old lady. She looked the porter in the eye.

"Now, see here, young man. That dog has walked twenty miles from St Killan to get to my granddaughter. Heaven knows how he knew she was here, but it's plain he knows. And he ought to have his rights! He ought to get to see her! Do you know," she went on, bristling, "that dog has walked the length of England—*twice*—to be with that girl? And you think you can keep him out with your fiddling rules and regulations?"

"I'll have to ask the medical officer," the porter said weakly.

"You do that, young man." Granny Pearce sat down in a determined manner, shutting her umbrella, and Lob sat patiently dripping at her feet. Every now and then he shook his head, as if to dislodge something heavy that was tied around his neck.

Presently a tired, thin, intelligent-looking man in a white coat came downstairs, with an impressive, silver-haired man in a dark suit, and there was a low-voiced discussion. Granny Pearce eyed them, biding her time.

"Frankly . . . not much to lose," said the older man. The man in the white coat approached Granny Pearce.

"It's strictly against every rule, but as it's such a serious case we are making an exception," he said to her quietly. "But only *outside* her bedroom door—and only for a moment or two."

Without a word, Granny Pearce rose and stumped upstairs. Lob followed close to her skirts, as if he knew his hope lay with her.

They waited in the green-floored corridor outside Sandy's room. The door was half shut. Bert and Jean were inside. Everything was terribly quiet. A nurse came out. The white-coated man asked her something and she shook her head. She had left the door ajar and through it could now be seen a high, narrow bed with a lot of gadgets around it. Sandy lay there, very flat under the covers, very still. Her head was turned away. All Lob's attention was riveted on the bed. He strained towards it, but Granny Pearce clasped his collar firmly.

"I've done a lot for you, my boy, now you behave yourself," she whispered grimly. Lob let out a faint whine, anxious and pleading.

At the sound of that whine Sandy stirred just a little. She sighed and moved her head the least fraction. Lob whined again. And then Sandy turned her head right over. Her eyes opened, looking at the door.

"Lob?" she murmured—no more than a breath of sound. "Lobby, boy?"

The doctor by Granny Pearce drew a quick, sharp breath. Sandy moved her left arm—the one that was not broken—from below the covers and let her hand dangle down, feeling, as she always did in the mornings, for Lob's furry head. The doctor nodded slowly.

93

"All right," he whispered. "Let him go to the bedside. But keep a hold of him."

Granny Pearce and Lob moved to the bedside. Now she could see Bert and Jean, white-faced and shocked, on the far side of the bed. But she didn't look at them. She looked at the smile on her granddaughter's face, as the groping fingers found Lob's wet ears and gently pulled them. "Good boy," whispered Sandy, and fell asleep again.

Granny Pearce led Lob out into the passage again. There she let go of him and he ran off swiftly down the stairs. She would have followed him, but Bert and Jean had come out into the passage, and she spoke to Bert fiercely.

"*I* don't know why you were so foolish as not to bring the dog before! Leaving him to find the way here himself—"

"But, Mother!" said Jean Pengelly. "That can't have been Lob. What a chance to take! Suppose Sandy hadn't—" She stopped, with her handkerchief pressed to her mouth.

"Not Lob? I've known that dog nine years! I suppose I ought to know my own granddaughter's dog?"

"Listen, Mother," said Bert. "Lob was killed by the same lorry that hit Sandy. Don found him—when he went to look for Sandy's schoolbag. He was—he was dead. Ribs all smashed. No question of that. Don told me on the phone—he and Will Hoskins rowed a half-mile out to sea, and sank the dog with a lump of concrete tied to his collar. Poor old boy. Still—he was getting on. Couldn't have lasted forever."

"*Sank him at sea?* Then what—?"

Slowly old Mrs Pearce, and then the other two, turned to look at the trail of dripping-wet footprints that led down the hospital stairs.

In the Pengellys' garden they have a stone, under the palm tree. It says: 'Lob. Sandy's dog. Buried at sea.'

The Last Specimen

The Reverend Matthew Greenheart, aged seventy, had a regular monthly habit. On his way to conduct Evensong in the tiny church of St-Anthony-under-the-Downs, he invariably parked his aged Rover for ten minutes by the side of a small patch of woodland about ten minutes' drive from the church.

Services at St Anthony's took place only once a month; for the rest of the time the isolated building with its Saxon stonework, Douai font, wilful harmonium and two massive yew trees, drowsed undisturbed, save by casual tourists who occasionally wandered in, looked around, dropped a ten pence piece into the box that begged help for the fabric of the roof, and inspected the small overgrown churchyard with its nineteen graves.

At the monthly services the congregation seldom exceeded half a dozen, and in wet weather or snow Mr Greenheart, and Miss Sedom who played the harmonium, had the place to themselves. St Anthony's lay three quarters of a mile from any house; the mild slopes of the Berkshire downs enfolded it as sometimes after a falling tide a cup of sand will hold a single pebble.

One of the Rector's favourite views was that of the church's swaybacked stone roof, bracketed between its two majestic dark yew trees, with the leisurely grey-green of the hillsides beyond. This was one reason for his pre-Evensong period of meditation beside the little wood. The second reason was the tactful desire to allow his parishioners time to assemble, sit down, and rest from their cross-country walk for a few minutes before he appeared among them. Except for the trees on his left, the countryside hereabouts lay bare as an open hand, so that the members of the congregation could be seen from a great distance, making their way along the footpath which led to the church from Compton Druce, the nearest hamlet.

On this evening in mid-April, Mr Greenheart sat in his rusty Rover with an especially happy and benign expression on his face. After a rainy afternoon the sky had cleared: thrushes, larks, and blackbirds were singing in fervent appreciation of the sun's last rays, which turned the greenish-white pearls of the budding hawthorn to a silvery dazzle. In this light the down grass and young wheat shone with an almost luminous intensity of colour.

"Interesting," mused Mr Greenheart, "how these early greens of the year, dog's mercury and elder leaves, and the green of bluebells, contain such a strong mixture of blue in their colour."

Mr Greenheart's hobby was painting delicate watercolour landscapes, and he was minutely observant of such niceties.

"Then later in the spring, in May and June, the brighter, more yellowy greens appear: young beech and oak leaves with their buttery rich colour; doubtless the extra degree of light from the sun has something to do with it."

Mr Greenheart watched fondly as Ben Tracey, the farmer who owned the enormous pasture on his right, arrived in a Landrover with sacks of feed for the sheep. The spring had been an unusually cold one, and the grass remained unseasonably scanty. Sighting Ben, the sheep and lambs, well acquainted with the object of his daily visit, began purposefully making towards him from all corners of the vast field, lambs following their mothers like iron filings drawn to a magnet in regular converging lines, only broken at one point by the presence of a massive oak tree covered with reddish buds which grew towards the middle of the field. Mr Greenheart eyed the tree thoughtfully. Was it not unusually forward in its growth for such a cold season? And why had he not noticed it last month?

Farmer and rector waved to one another, then Mr Greenheart, observing the last of his congregation pass through the churchyard and enter St Anthony's porch, was about to start his motor again, when, in the rear-view mirror, he noticed a girl, who had been slowly riding her pony along the road behind the car. At this moment she dismounted, tethered the pony to a tree, and vanished through a gate into the little wood.

Normally such a sight would have aroused no particular curiosity in Mr Greenheart, but two unusual factors here caught his attention. First, neither girl nor mount were familiar to him; yet Mr Greenheart was certain that he knew every girl and every pony within a ten-mile radius. The population in this district was very scanty. Everybody knew everybody else. So where had the girl come from? Secondly, she carried a trowel and a basket.

Without apparent haste, yet acting with remarkable calm and dispatch for a man of his age, Mr Greenheart backed the Rover a hundred yards to the point where the pony stood tethered to a young ash tree. The Rector got out of his car, studied the pony thoughtfully for a moment, then walked into the wood. The gate stood open: another factor worthy of note. Slightly compressing his lips, Mr Greenheart closed it behind him, and took the path that bisected the wood. The girl ahead of him was easily visible because of her bright blue anorak; she was, in any case, walking slowly, glancing from side to side as if in search of something.

Mr Greenheart could easily guess at the object of her quest. He caught up with her just as she had reached it: a patch of delicate spindly plants, each of them nine inches to a foot high, growing in a small sunny clearing. They had bell-shaped flowers the size of small, upside-down tulips—odd, elegant, mysterious flowers: white, with a pinkish-purple tracery over the fluted petals.

The girl knelt beside them and took her trowel from the basket.

"No, no. You mustn't," said Mr Greenheart gently behind her. The girl gasped and spun round, gazing up at him with wide, frightened eyes.

"My dear child, believe me, you *mustn't*," repeated the Rector, the seriousness of his tone mitigated to some degree by the mild expression in his blue eyes. The girl gazed at him, nonplussed, embarrassed, temporarily speechless, it seemed.

She was, he noticed, a very pretty girl, about seventeen, perhaps, in the accustomed uniform of jeans and T-shirt and riding boots. On her head, though, she sported a slightly absurd and certainly unusual article of headgear—not a crash helmet, but a strapped furry hat with a cylindrical top, like the shakoes worn by cavalry in the Crimean war. Could she have inherited it from some great-great grandfather? Or perhaps, thought the Vicar indulgently, it was a prop borrowed from some local theatrical venture; the young loved to get themselves up in fancy dress. But, now that he saw her close to, he knew that he did not know this girl; she was a total stranger. Her eyes were a clear beautiful greenish gold—like the colour of the young oak leaves he had been

98

thinking about a few minutes earlier. Her hair, what could be seen of it under the shako, was the same colour, with a decided greenish tint; punk, no doubt, thought Mr Greenheart knowledgeably. The children nowadays dyed their hair extraordinary colours; green was nothing out of the common. He had seen pink, orange and lilac.

The girl continued to gaze at him in silence, abashed and nervous, grasping her trowel.

"Wild fritillaries are so rare, so very rare," Mr Greenheart mildly explained to her, "that it is wrong, it is most dreadfully wrong to dig them up; besides, of course, being against the law. Did you not know that? And why, do you suppose, are they so rare?" he went on, considerately giving her time to recover her composure. "Why, because of people like yourself, my dear, finding out about where they grow, and coming to dig up specimens. I know the temptation—believe me, I know it!—but you really must *not*, you know."

"Oh dear," murmured the girl, finding her voice at last, it seemed. "I'm—I'm very sorry. I—I didn't know."

"No? You really didn't know? Where are you from?" he inquired, gently veiling his disbelief. "You are certainly not from anywhere around here, or I should have known you. And your steed," he added thoughtfully.

"No, I—I come from—from quite a long way away. I was sent . . ." she hesitated, looking sheepish and contrite, "sent to—to collect a specimen, as you say. It is the last, you see. We already have one of everything else."

Good gracious, thought Mr Greenheart, in surprise and a certain amount of disapproval. *Everything* else? Aloud he said,

"It is for a school project, I conclude? Well, I am sorry to disappoint you, but you really must *not* remove the flowers from this precious patch. I will tell you what you can do, though—" as her face fell. "If you care to accompany me to

Evensong in St Anthony's—or, of course, wait outside the church if you prefer—" he added kindly, "you may then come with me to my Rectory in Chilton Parsley. I am fortunate enough to have quite a large number of fritillaries growing in my flower border, and I shall be happy to give you a specimen for your collection. How about that, my dear?"

"Why," said the girl slowly, "that—that is very kind of Your Reverence. I am indeed greatly obliged to you." She spoke with considerable formality; although English enough in appearance, she could, judging from her accent, have been a foreigner who had learned the language very correctly from some aristocratic old lady with nineteenth-century intonations. "I have instructions to be back though," she glanced at the sky, then at the watch on her wrist, "by seven. Will that—?"

"Plenty of time," he assured her, smiling. "The evening service is never a long one. Strict about that sort of thing, are they, at your school?"

She blushed.

Mr Greenheart began walking back towards the gate, anxious, without making it too obvious that he was in a hurry, to join his patient parishioners, but also wishful to be certain that the girl accompanied him. She, however, showed no sign of intending to disobey his probibition, and came with him biddably enough. Once outside the copse gate—"You must *always* close gates, you know," Mr Greenheart reminded her amiably but firmly—she remounted, and he got into his car. "Just follow behind," he told her, poking his white-haired head out of the window. She nodded, kicking the shaggy pony into a walk; perhaps it was the late light filtered through the young hawthorns, but the pony, too, Mr Greenheart thought, showed a decided touch of green in its rough coat. "Only a very short way to the church," he called, swerving his car erratically across the road as he put his head out again to impart this information.

The girl nodded and kicked her pony again. For its diminutive size—a Shetland cross, perhaps?—the pony certainly showed a remarkable turn of speed.

Mr Greenheart had not expected that the girl would be prepared to attend his service, but she quietly tied her pony to the lych gate, murmured some exhortation into its ear, and followed him through the churchyard, glancing about her with interest. Then a doubt seemed to overtake her: "Am I dressed suitably to come inside?" she asked in a low, worried tone, pausing at the church door.

"Perfectly," he assured her, smiling at the glossy shako. "Our congregation at St Anthony's is quite informal."

So she slipped in after him and demurely took her place in a pew at the back. After the service—which, as he had promised, lasted no longer than twenty-five minutes—the Rector exchanged a few friendly words with the six members of his congregation, stood waving goodbye to them as they set off on their return walk across the fields, and then said to the girl, who had remounted and was waiting by the gate:

"Now, if you will follow me again, my dear, I will drive slowly, and I do not think the journey should take more than about fifteen minutes for that excellent little animal of yours."

She nodded, and they proceeded as before, the Vicar driving at twenty miles an hour, not much less than his normal speed, while horse and rider followed with apparent ease.

As he drove, Mr Greenheart reflected. During Evensong his mind, as always, had been entirely given over to the service, but he had, with some part of it, heard the girl's voice now and then, particularly in the hymn (Miss Sedom's favourite) 'Glory to thee my God this night'. So the girl was, at least, familiar with Christian ritual. Or was a remarkably speedy learner. Or, was it conceivable that she could be coached, as it were, continuously by—by whatever agency had sent her? There were so many things wrong with her—and yet, mused the Rector, he could swear that there was no harm about her, not an atom.

When they reached the damp and crumbling laurel-girt Rectory, Mr Greenheart drove round, as was his habit, to the mossy yard to the rear, and parked there.

"You can tie your pony to the mounting block—" he gestured to the old stable. "Now, I will just leave my cassock inside the back door—so—and fetch a trowel—ah, no, of course there is no need for that, you already have one." It was a bricklayer's trowel, but no matter. "Follow me, then."

The Rectory garden, beyond the overgrown laurel hedge, was a wonderful wilderness of old-fashioned flowers and shrubs which had grown, proliferated and battled for mastery during the last hundred years. Smaller and more delicate plants had, on the whole, fared badly; but Mr Greenheart adored his fritillaries and had cherished them as carefully as he was able: frail and beautiful, both speckled and white, they drooped their magic bells among a drift of pale blue anemones and a fringe of darker blue grape hyacinths.

"Aren't they extraordinary?" he said, fondly looking down at them. "It is so easy to believe in a benevolent Creator when one considers these and the anemones—which, I believe, are the Lilies of the Field referred to by St Matthew. Now, this little clump, still in bud, would, I think transfer without too much harm, my dear—er—what did you say your name was?"

She hesitated. Then, "My name is Anjla," she answered, with a slight, uneasy tremor in her voice. And she knelt to dig up the clump of plants he had indicated. The Rector fetched her a grimy plastic bag from the toolshed, but she shook her head.

"Thank you, but I can't take it. Only the flowers. This is—this is truly very kind of you."

A faint warning hum sounded in the air—like that of a clock before it strikes.

The Vicar glanced across the wide meadow which lay alongside his garden. A large oak, leafless still, covered with reddish buds, grew in the middle of the grassy space. Mr Greenheart eyed it thoughtfully. Beyond it, pale and clear, shone the evening star.

Mr Greenheart said, "My dear—where do you really come from?"

The girl stood, tucking the plants into her basket. She followed the direction of his glance, but said, defensively, "You would not know the name of the place."

It was, however, remarkably hard to evade Mr Greenheart when he became as serious as he was now.

"Forgive my curiosity," he said, "but I do think it important that I should know—precisely why are you collecting specimens?"

She was silent for a moment; for too long. Mr Greenheart went on, "You see—I am an absent-minded, vague old man, but even I could not help noticing that your pony has claws on its hoofs. Moropus! A prehistoric horse not seen in these parts for thirty million years! And, well, there were various other things . . ."

She blushed furiously.

"That was the trouble!" she burst out. "For such a small errand—just one flower—they wouldn't allocate enough research staff. I *knew* there were details they had scamped on—"

"But why," he persisted mildly, "why are you collecting?"

103

Anjla looked at him sorrowfully. Then she said, "Well, as you seem to have spotted us, and, in any case, it is so very late, I suppose it won't matter now if I tell you . . ."

"Yes, my dear?"

"This planet—" she glanced round at the stable yard "—is due to blow up—oh, very, very soon. Our scientists have calculated it to within the next three chronims—"

"Chronims?"

"Under one hundred of your hours, I think. Naturally, therefore, we were checking the contents of our own Terrestrial Museum—"

"Ah, I see." He stood thinking for a few minutes, then inquired with the liveliest interest, "And you really do have one of everything? Even, for instance, a rector of the Church of England?"

"I'm afraid so." Her tone was full of regret. "I *wish* I could take you with me. You have been so kind. But we have a vicar, a dean, a bishop, a canon—we have them all. Even an archbishop."

"My dear child! You mistook my meaning. I would not, not for one moment, consider leaving. My question was prompted by—by a simple wish to know—"

The low hum was audible again. Anjla glanced at the sky.

"I'm afraid that now I really have to go."

"Of course you must, my dear. Of course."

They crossed the yard, and found the shaggy Moropus demolishing, with apparent relish, the last of a bunch of carrots which had been laid on the mounting block for Mr Greenheart's supper.

Anjla checked and stared, aghast.

"*Sphim!* What have you *done?*"

She burst into a torrent of expostulation, couched in a language wholly unlike any earthly tongue; it appeared to have no consonants at all, to consist of pure sound, like the breathy note of an ocarina.

The Moropus guiltily hung its head and shuffled its long-clawed feet.

Mr Greenheart stood looking at the pair in sympathy and perplexity.

The warning hum sounded in the air again.

"Do I understand that your—um—companion has in-validated his chance of departure by the consumption of those carrots?"

"I don't know what *can* have come over him—we were briefed so carefully, told to touch nothing, to take in nothing except . . . over and over again they told us—"

"Perhaps it was a touch of Method," suggested Mr Greenheart. "He was really getting into the skin of his part." And he added something about Dis and Persephone which the girl received with the blankness of non-comprehension. She had placed her hands on either side of the pony's hairy cheekbones; she bent forward until her forehead touched the other's. Thus she stood for a couple of moments in silence. Then, she straightened and walked across the yard in the direction of the meadow. Her eyes swam with tears. Following her, interested and touched, Mr Greenheart murmured,

"I will, of course, be glad to take care of your friend. During what little time remains."

"I am sure that you will. Thank you. I—I am glad to have met you."

"You could not, I suppose, show me what you both really look like?" he asked with a touch of wistfulness.

"I'm afraid that would be quite impossible. Your eyes simply aren't adapted, you see . . ."

He nodded, accepting this. Just the same, for a single

instant, he did receive an impression of hugeness, brightness, speed. Then the girl vaulted the fence and, carefully carrying her basket, crossed the meadow to the large oak tree in the centre.

"Goodbye," called Mr Greenheart. The Moropus lifted up its head and let out a soft groaning sound.

Beside the oak tree, Anjla turned and raised her hand with a grave, formal gesture. Then she stepped among the low-growing branches of the tree, which immediately folded like an umbrella and, with a swift flash of no-coloured brilliance, shot upwards, disintegrating into light.

Mr Greenheart remained, for a few moments, leaning with his forearms on the wooden fence and gazing pensively at the star Hesperus, which, now that the tree was gone, could be seen gleaming in radiance above the horizon.

The Rector murmured,

> Earth's joys grow dim, its glories pass away
> Change and decay in all around I see;
> O Thou, Who changest not, abide with me.

Then, pulling a juicy tussock of grass from beside one of the fence-posts, he carried it back to the disconsolate Moropus.

"Here, my poor friend; if we are to wait for Armageddon together, we may as well do so in comfort. Just excuse me for a moment while I fetch a deck chair and a steamer rug from the house. And do, pray, finish those carrots. I will be with you again directly."

He stepped inside the back door. The Moropus, with a carrot-top and a hank of juicy grass dangling from its hairy lips, gazed after him sadly but trustfully.

The Lame King

"Crumbling rainbows are useless as a diet," said Mrs Logan. "I don't like 'em. Prefer something solid to bite on."

Under her breath, in the front passenger's seat, Mrs Logan's daughter-in-law, Sandra, muttered, "Shut up, you dotty old bore." And, above her breath, she added to her husband, "*Can't* you drive a bit faster, Philip? It will be terribly late by the time we get home. There's the sitter's fee, don't forget. And we've got all our packing to do."

"You have all tomorrow to do it in," her father-in-law mildly pointed out from the back seat. She flashed him an angry diagonal glance, and snapped,

"There's plenty of other things to do, as well as packing. Cancel the milk, take Buster to the Dog's Hotel, fill out all the notification forms—"

"I would have done that, if you had let me," said old Mr Logan in his precise tones. He had been a headmaster. Sandra made no answer at all to this, merely pressed her lips tight together and clenched her gloved hands in her lap. "Do drive faster, Philip," she said again.

Philip frowned and slightly shook his head, without taking his eyes off the road. He was tall and pale, with a bony, righteous face and eyes like faded olives. "Can't; you know that perfectly well; it's illegal to go over sixty with Senior

107

Citizens in the car," he said in a low voice. His remark was drowned, anyway, by the voice of his mother, old Mrs Logan, who called from the back:

"Oh no, don't drive faster, Philip dear, please don't drive any faster! I am so *loving* the landscape—I don't want to lose a moment of it! Our heroine, speeding to who knows where, or what destination, is reminded of childhood—those bare trees, the spring mornings passed paddling in brooks when the water went over the tops of your wellies, the empty fields—"

Old Mr Logan gently took her hand in his, which had the effect of checking her.

"It *is* a pretty country," he said. "I like all the sheep. And the shapes of the hills around here."

"How much farther?" said Sandra to her husband.

"About another four hours' driving. We'd better stop for a snack at a Cooks' Tower."

"Oh, why?" Sandra said crossly, in a low tone. "It's just a waste of money giving them a—"

"No wolves now. It must have been so exciting for shepherds in the old days," dreamily remarked old Mrs Logan. "Virginia came down like a wolf on the . . . but then when you try and fold on the dotted line it *never* tears straight. That is one thing they should put right in the next world."

"And I'm sure they will," said her husband comfortingly.

"I hope my thoughts are not without sense."

"Never to me, my love. Look at that farm, tucked so snugly in the hollow."

"Will the place we are going to be like that?"

"Anyway the tank needs filling," said Philip to his wife.

"What this trip will have *cost*," she muttered.

"It had to be taken some time. And we'll get the Termination Grants, don't forget," Philip reminded his wife in a murmur.

"Well, but then you have to deduct all the expenses . . ."

"Sometimes I think my daughter-in-law treads in the footsteps of Sycorax," absently remarked old Mrs Logan, who sometimes caught Sandra's tone, though not the things she actually said.

"Oh come, you would hardly call little Kevin a Caliban?" her husband remonstrated mildly.

"Parting from little Kevin is the least of my regrets. He is all the chiefs and none of the Indians. And stubborn! Combs his hair five times and then says 'I don't want to go'."

"Kevin will grow up by and by. If he were a character in one of your books, you would know how to make him grow up."

"Ah," she said with a sigh, "no story would grow in my hands now. It would fly apart in a cloud of feathers. You say a few words—and they come back and hit you like boomerangs. What did Western man do before he knew about the boomerang? What did swallows do before they invented telegraph wires? Language is so inexact—I do not mean to assert that the swallows themselves invented the wires—"

"For God's *sake*, shut up," muttered young Mrs Logan in the front seat. Old Mr Logan laid an arm protectively round his wife's shoulders. She, with an alert, happy face, white hair flying about in wisps, continually gazed out of the window as the car sped along. "Haven't seen so much grass in ten years," she whispered. Her elderly husband looked at her calmly and fondly. Sometimes a shadow of pain flitted across his face, like that of a high jet over a huge field, but it was gone the moment after.

"There's a place," said Philip. "We'll stop there."

A Cook's Tower had come in sight: square white pillar, castellated at the top, with red zig-zags all the way down, and a wide car park glittering with massed vehicles.

"Park somewhere close in; we don't want to waste twenty minutes helping them hobble," muttered Sandra.

"I'll park as close as I can," replied Philip with a frown, and called to the pair in the back, "Fancy a snack, Mum and Dad? Cup o' tea? Sandwich?"

He tried to make his voice festive.

"Oh, there's no need for that, my boy," said his father. "We're all right, we're not hungry. Save your money." But his mother called, "Oh yes! A nice cup of tea and a last rock cake. Rock of ages cleft for me . . . A book called *The Last Rock Cake*, now—that would have been a certain seller, once; these days, I suppose, *The Last Croissant*. Take the Queen en croissant; a husband in Bohemia would be a Czech mate. Oh, cries his poor silly wife, I am nothing but a blank Czeque; good for nothing but to be wheeled away to the Death House."

"*Will* you be quiet, Mother?" gritted Sandra, turning to the rear of the car a face of real ferocity.

"Never mind, my dear, you won't have us for much longer. It has been a stony row, I know, but tomorrow this time you will be en route for Ibiza—"

Philip, who had been weaving watchfully through the car park, eyes veering sharply this way and that, now whipped his Algonquin neatly into a just-vacated gap close to the main entrance.

Inside, at this time of day, the Quik-Snak cafeteria was half empty; most customers were up on the top floor having the Three Course Special.

"You sit here."

Philip edged his parents alongside a glass-topped table by the window.

"Sandra and I will forage at the counter. What's it to be? Buttered toast?"

110

"A rock cake," sighed Mrs Logan. "Just a rock cake. To remind me of our honeymoon in Lynmouth."

Mr Logan said he wanted nothing but a cup of tea. He placed a careful hand to his side. Mrs Logan noticed this and sighed again, but said nothing.

Their table was littered with crumby plates, crumpled paper napkins, half-empty cups, and, on the windowsill, a grease-smeared, dog-eared paperback.

"Why, look, my dear," said old Mr Logan, turning it over. "It's one of yours. *The Short Way Back*. Now, isn't that a remarkable coincidence. A good omen, wouldn't you say?"

They gazed at each other, delighted.

"I was only twenty-five when I wrote that one," sighed his wife. "Philip already on the way . . . How could I *do* it? What came into my head? *Now*, I couldn't . . ."

She handled the book gently, affectionately, smiling at the absurd picture on the front.

"Nothing at all to do with what's inside. But then, whatever is?"

A small old man, limping, passed by their table. His heavy metal tray held a glass of stout, black, froth-topped, and a shiny Bath bun.

"*That* looks good," said Mrs Logan to him confidentially. "Now I'm sorry I didn't ask for stout. And a Bath bun . . . Do you know what? We found, we actually found a book I once wrote, lying here on the windowsill. Now isn't that a thing!"

"Well I never!" The man with the stout beamed at her. "So you're a book-writer, are you?" His voice had a slight regional burr. Welsh? wondered Mr Logan. Or Scottish?

"Was once. In those *jeunesse dorée* days. Do re me, lackaday dee—" she sung softly.

" 'He sipped no sup and he craved no crumb,' " joined in the old man with the tray, " 'as he sighed for the love of a lady.' "

"Why!" exclaimed Mrs Logan in astonished pleasure. "Now you remind me—you remind me of somebody I once knew—"

"I was just thinking the very same thing!" said her husband. "But who—?"

All three looked at one another in excitement and suspense.

"Now, when was it, where was it?" murmured Mrs Logan.

But at this moment Philip came back with a tray, followed by Sandra, with another.

"Excuse *me*," he said with brisk chill, and the old man with the stout moved quickly on his way.

"*Really*, Mother," snapped Sandra, "must you get into conversation with all and sundry?" And she thumped down in front of her mother-in-law a thick china plate on which lay a flat pale macaroon, ninety-percent grey pastry, with a flat wan dob of fawn-coloured substance in the middle.

"Oh, but I asked for a rock cake. This isn't—"

"No rock cakes. Only jam tarts, buns or macaroons."

Mrs Logan drank her tea but declined the macaroon. "Too hard on my teeth. *You* have it, love." So Philip ate it, after his ham roll, with a harassed air of doing so only because it had been paid for and must not go to waste. Sandra nibbled a salad which was largely cress. She looked repeatedly at her watch.

"Philip, we should be getting on. Need the Ladies, Mother? You better, you don't know what there will be at—"

Rather reluctantly Mrs Logan rose to her feet and followed her daughter-in-law to the pink boudoir, peppered over with hearts and cupids.

"Sandra," she said—for the first time a slight tremor entered her voice—"Sandra, will it be *frightening*, do you think—where we're going?"

Sandra angrily banged at her nose with a make-up puff and skated a comb through her perm. "Frightening? Why should it? Everyone's got to go through it some time, haven't they? Not just you. We'll have to, too, Philip and me, when our turn comes. There's nothing *frightening* about it. Come along, the others will be waiting. Hurry up!"

Philip and his father waited at the window table. Philip had impatiently piled together all the used cups, plates, napkins, and the paperback book, without observing its title.

"Women take so long, always," he muttered. "Can't think what they get up to."

The limping old man passed their table again and nodded in a friendly way at Mr Logan.

"On the way to Last House, are you?"

"Why should you ask that?" said Philip sharply.

"Many who stop here are going that way. There's a bad greasy patch at the S-bend going over Endby Hill: you want to watch it there. Quite a few have come off at that corner."

"Thank you," said old Mr Logan. "We'll remember."

Philip gave a curt nod, as if he needed no lame old strangers to teach him about careful driving, and Mr Logan added cheerfully,

"It'd be a piece of irony, wouldn't it, if just when you were taking us—*there*—we all went off the road and ended up together!"

"Father! *Really!*"

"Little Kevin would have to go into an orphanage."

"Here come the girls," said Philip, with a jocularity he did not feel.

"What's that about an orphanage?" inquired his mother,

113

who, her husband noticed, had a drawn and anxious look on her face. She plunged into the conversation as if trying to distract her own mind. "They say many a home is worse than an orphanage. Remember, some also agree that impatience is the worst sin. I suffered from it myself, to an extreme degree, when I was young . . ."

"Come along, let's go," said Philip, showing signs of suffering from the worst sin himself.

A frail dusk had begun to fall as they resumed their journey. The landscape became ghostly, wreathed in layers of mist. Trees loomed, fringed by creepers, then swung past; the road wound uphill through forest.

"I wonder if there will be a view?" murmured old Mrs Logan, more to herself than to her companions. Her husband took her hand, holding it close and firmly. She went on, still to herself, "He was always delighted with your comments on landscape, chaffinches, and so forth; I wonder if he would be still? That was a curious encounter, a curious coincidence. Candied apple, quince and plum, and gourd . . . I wonder what candied *gourd* would be like? Not very nice, I'd think. But then the whole of that picnic sounded decidedly sickly—lucent syrops tinct with cinnamon: *not* what one would wish on one's bed in the middle of the night."

"Please be quiet, mother," said Philip edgily. "There's a bad place along here, we were warned about it: I don't want any distraction, if you would be so kind."

"Of course, Philip, of course. I am so very sorry, I know I am a nuisance to you."

The bad place was negotiated, and passed, in complete silence. The elderly pair in the back drew close together in the darkness until they seemed like one person. The headlights in front drew to a sharp white V through the foggy murk.

114

At last the car rolled to a stop.

"Is this the place?" Mrs Logan's voice quivered a very little.

"This is it."

Philip, relieved at having completed the outward trip, stamped to get the stiffness out of his knees; his voice was rather too cheerful. "Come along, Mother, Dad; we'll just get you registered, then we must be on our way; we're going to have to hurry to get home by the time the sitter wants to leave—"

The old people crept awkwardly out from the back of the car.

"One thing, there's no luggage to bother about," muttered Sandra. "But you would think they'd make these places more accessible—"

The small group of persons passed inside a building which was so closely surrounded by creeper-hung trees of large size that, in the foggy dark, no architectural detail was visible; it was like walking into a grove, Mrs Logan thought.

The elderly pair clung together, hand clasped tightly in hand, while forms were filled out at the desk.

Then—

"Well, we'll be leaving you now, then, Mum and Dad," said Philip, falsely hearty. "Cheerio! Take care! All the best. Bon voyage, and all that." He gave them each a peck on the cheek. Sandra muttered something inaudible, and the younger pair walked hastily out though the front entrance.

"Whooo!" Philip muttered, after a moment, slamming the car into gear. "Wouldn't want to go through *that* again in a hurry."

"Now," hissed his wife, "now will you *please* drive at a reasonable speed? No more dawdling, if you please. There's a whole *lot* to do when we get home."

115

"All right, all right—" and he accelerated so sharply that the engine let out a squawk of protest.

Old Mr and Mrs Logan were led in different directions.

"But can't we be together?" she protested.

"No. We are very sorry, but that is an absolute rule. There is nothing to worry about, though . . ."

They gave each other a cold, steady kiss, aged cheek against soft aged cheek.

"Now then, where?"

Mrs Logan was taken to a kind of garden room. One wall was totally lacking; darkness, trees, and mist lay beyond the area of dim illumination.

"If you wouldn't mind just waiting here . . . He won't be long."

"Will it be Ted's turn first, or mine?"

No answer came back. Or had the guide perhaps said, "Both together?" as the door closed?

Mrs Logan sat on a bench, looking out anxiously into the dark.

It isn't very cold, she thought. Not as cold as you'd expect. Not cold at all, really. Cold blows the wind tonight, true love . . . Wasn't that queer, though, finding that book? Then tell to me, my own true love, when shall we meet again? When the autumn leaves that fall from the trees, are green and spring again. Yes, but *do* they spring again? Leaves, like the things of man you with your fresh thoughts care for, can you? Always dwell as if about to depart, they say in Yorkshire. Do they depart so easily, up there in Yorkshire? Questions are better than answers, for they lead you on, like signposts, whereas answers pin you down, like javelins. Will Ted remember to tell them about his diet?

Somebody was approaching through the darkness, walking

116

slowly and carefully; the sound of the footfalls came with an irregular beat, as if the person limped.

Vulcan, thought Mrs Logan; Richard III. 'Beware the lame king, for then shall Sparta fall. But the lame god is kind, he knows our frailties all . . .' that line does not scan as it should. One foot too many, like a three-legged stool. Or too few . . .

"There you are, then," said the old lame man. "I brought you a glass of stout; and a Bath bun."

"So it was you, all along?"

She gazed at him in amazement.

"All along."

"All along," she echoed happily, "down along, out along lee."

"That's it!"

And they began to sing together, their voices combining gently in old, remembered, graceful cadences. Oh, I hope Ted is as happy as this! she thought.

Far away from Endby Hill, the sound of a long drawn out crash came faintly though the foggy dark. But neither of the singers paid it any heed.

Homer's Whistle

I had always known Homer Peasmarsh. We were together
and friendly all through our first school. He was the small
silent boy with straight-cut fringe of fair, almost cotton-white,
hair, and round intent grey-blue eyes, who arrived in a
brand-new school uniform somewhat too big for him,
clutching a tortoise. Nobody else had a tortoise, so that put up
his stock at once. His grandmother had given it to him. She
gave him amazing presents with which he came back at the
beginning of every term. And, during the term also, bulging,
untidily wrapped parcels would arrive from her, and inside
them would be crumbling, delicious home-made cakes, or
books, marbles, a dagger, some coins—not many of these
things, but each of them rare and special. Once she sent him a
watch strap made from elephants' hairs; once, two enormous
butterflies in glass cases. Once, a telescope.

In the holidays he generally went to stay with his
grandmother because his parents travelled a great deal. And
even when his parents were at home it seemed they did not get
on together; they lived in separate places and could not agree
which one Homer should stay with first. In fact they disliked
each other so much that they could not even bear to meet
when Homer had to be transferred from his father to his
mother, so often he would be left standing on the pavement

for an hour or so waiting for the other parent to turn up.

In those days I liked Homer very much. Partly, of course, because of the interesting things his grandmother sent. Partly because, in the summer, I was sometimes invited to stay at her cottage in Devon, which was just below the edge of the moor, between a rocky brook and a river the colour of milkless tea. Besides these things, I liked Homer because his mind was deep and clear. He never made pretences. Never told lies. His thoughts came out, plain and simple. If he had nothing to say, he kept silent.

So we were friends through the years at our small private prep school, which was called Hollyhaw. And when Homer's grandmother discovered that I had been put down for Watchetts, she persuaded his father to send Homer there too. "His friend Andrew is a decent sort of boy," I suppose she said. "Homer doesn't have much family life, it would be better if he went on through schooldays with his friend."

Around that time Homer's parents finally got divorced; one of them went to live in Brazil, the other in the south of France. So you could say that he had no family life at all. Also, not long after that, Homer's grandmother died. I think she had known that she was going to die for about a year beforehand. And, shortly before her death, the small valley below the moor had a dam thrown across its lower end, was filled up with water from the river, and turned into a reservoir. Homer's grandmother's cottage was the only home affected. It now lies thirty feet under water, with weeds growing on its chimneys and fish swimming through its broken windows. I rather hate to think of it.

Drowning the cottage did upset Homer very badly. He had always been a little afraid of deep water. He used to like playing in the brook, and splashing in the shallower parts of the river. But he took care to avoid the deep stretches.

Sometimes, after a heavy rain up on the moor, the river did a thing we called 'coming down'; a great bolster of brown water would roll swiftly along, gathering size and speed on its way, and crash over our little stone bridge. I loved to watch this, it was thrilling, but it made Homer slightly nervous, he worried about the likelihood of sheep and rabbits getting drowned; he much preferred the brook and river at their placid, chuckling, summertime levels.

After his grandmother's death, and the submerging of her cottage, he began having bad nightmares, and would wake screaming from some awful muddled vision of wicked broken brown water, foam and crumbling masonry.

Then we shifted from our small comfortable private prep school to the big, careless, rather tough public-school world of Watchetts, where, instead of being at the top of the school and greatly respected, we were just small fry, swimming for our lives among five hundred others.

What counted at Watchetts was whether you were good at sport. I enjoyed boxing and running and football, so I managed well enough and was accepted; but Homer had never been interested in games; his large grey-blue eyes were short-sighted and needed steel-framed glasses; he could not catch a ball, and was always afraid that his glasses would get broken (with some reason, for they often did). So he was universally despised. And he became almost completely silent, only uttering when a master asked him a question in class, and not always then.

"Wake up, Peasmarsh!" they would bark. "You're in a dream, as usual!" Sometimes Homer would respond, and sometimes he would seem too far off in his own remotenesses for any human voice to fetch him back.

Since his grandmother died, he had spent school holidays with a distantly connected uncle and aunt who lived in West

Kensington; they were very boring, he said, and so was their house, but they did leave him to his own devices most of the time, and he seemed to pass days and weeks on end in museums. I think he was very unhappy, both in term and holiday time, but the school terms were certainly worse, because the other boys used to bully him and call him 'Drip-drop' and the masters shouted at him.

I suppose I should have invited him to stay in the holidays, but I never did. Having him to stay in Colchester wouldn't be a bit the same as those idyllic visits at the cottage by the moor.

Homer was never much good at school work because so much of the time his attention seemed to be elsewhere.

"Why don't you ever pay attention in class?" I asked him once. "What in the world are you thinking about when you go off into one of those dreams of yours?"

"Eh? What? Oh, the cottage, of course. Downcombe," he answered vaguely. "Wishing I could get back there. Remember the Wuzzy, where we made such a lot of tunnels under the brambles? And the haybarn where we did acrobatics when it rained? And the summer we constructed dozens of artificial islands in the river and planted them with wild flowers? And the calves that we played bullfights with in the meadow? And the mushrooms we used to bring in, that Grandmother fried for supper? And the nuts in Tankerton Wood? I just wish I could go back there . . ."

"But you can't go back there now," I pointed out. "It's all under water. The whole place, Tankerton Wood and all."

"I know that," he answered rather crossly.

"Well then it seems to me pointless to think about it."

He muttered, "If only it were possible to get back there in the time before it was made into a lake. It had been there for hundreds of years. And, after all, time is only something *we* invented, for our own convenience. Like the Fahrenheit

121

scale. Heat and cold and time were there before we began measuring them. If only we could step outside the scale, outside of measured time, I bet it would be possible to go forward or back to any part we wanted to visit. I wouldn't want to go forward; I just want to go back."

"That's an idiotic way to talk. How could you possibly?"

I didn't mean to get angry with him, but it did make me mad to see him wasting his time so. He wasn't learning anything; he wasn't making friends; he wasn't making progress of any kind. When he could get away from people—which wasn't very often—he'd just sit in a corner, absolutely still, completely silent; he hardly seemed to be breathing. Just once in a way you'd see his nostrils flicker just a little, like the throat of a frog.

"Breathing control, and concentration, are very important. That's what would do it," he once absently remarked to me when we happened to sit side by side at school lunch. (We weren't seeing so much of each other now.) It was a treacle tart day and everyone else was bolting their helping in hope of seconds, while Homer let his piece go cold on its plate and seemed to be staring at something about a hundred miles beyond the school dining room window.

"Wake up, Drip-drop, Tideswell's pinched your pud!" somebody yelled; and Homer came slowly back from wherever he had been and muttered, "Pudding? Pudding? Oh, what does it matter, what's the difference?"

After a while I made another friend. I had found that it really didn't do to be seen about all the time with nobody but Homer. People began to think that I must be a bit retarded too, in spite of my playing in the lower school second eleven. So, after a few months, I began going round with a boy called Sparky Timms, who was pretty good at all games and could do funny imitations of TV personalities as well. At first Homer used to trail round after us rather forlornly, about four yards in the rear.

"What in the world do you see in that oaf?" he asked once, when Sparky was somewhere else and we happened to be alone together.

"He's funny. Why? Are you jealous?"

"*Jealous?* Good heavens, no. I just find him terribly boring."

"Well, I'm sorry," I said coldly, "but *I* happen to like him."

Of course now that Homer's grandmother was dead he no longer received those parcels of delicious cakes, obscure books with weird pictures, luminous Victorian glass marbles, pocket astrolabes, and Japanese shinto objects; in fact his possessions were now very dismal, because although the aunt and uncle in London doubtless meant well, his parents were so far out of reach that they were always behind with the money for his clothes and stuff he needed for school. So he looked shabby and uncared-for; his hair generally needed cutting, and his sleeves were far too short, and his toes poked through the canvas of his gym shoes. By now the gifts his grandmother had sent him at Hollyhaw were mostly lost or broken or given away (for he had always been generous with his things—I had been given quite a few of them); all that remained was a little old whistle, made of copper. It had a ring round it, halfway along, which you could twist, to make its tone shriller and shriller, until it finally reached the point where a human ear could not reach its note. Dogs and bats were still able to hear it then, Homer said, but I could never see the point of that. Who wants to whistle to a bat? It had belonged to a seventeenth-century astrologer and mathematician, Homer said, an Exeter-born man called Prester

Holinshed, who had written several books on the science of
numbers and related subjects. P. Holinshed believed that
when numbers reached a certain point of magnitude they
changed to something else, as ice changes to water and then to
steam at certain temperatures.

"Change to *what*?" I asked once, but Homer said
Holinshed did not seem to have carried his researches far
enough to come to any conclusion about what the next
step was after numbers. Holinshed had built the cottage,
Downcombe, where old Mrs Peasmarsh lived, and his whistle
had been discovered in a little niche to the side of the
mantelpiece beam; his initials, P.H., were carved on the
whistle, and the date, 1685. Homer loved the whistle because
the initials were his own, in reverse, and the date was nearly
three hundred years back.

At the beginning of one autumn term Sparky Timms came
back with a whole new batch of information about sex, which
he was in the middle of passing on to me when Homer
appeared looking paler, shabbier, odder, and more disconsolate then ever.

"I've got something to tell you," he muttered to me.

"Oh, do buzz off, Homer, can't you see I'm talking to
Sparky just now," I said, and, after a minute or two of
awkward hanging about in case I changed my mind, he left us
again with the kind of clumsy shambling lope which he had
developed as he grew larger.

"Why in the world don't you tell that dummy to go and
jump in the river?" said Sparky, and went on with what he
was telling me.

Slowly, after that, a change began to be observable in
Homer. Very probably nobody noticed it but me. I was the
only person who troubled to take notice of him.

These days, even more of the time, he seemed to be lost in a total dream; but, oddly enough, even while he was in the dream, he seemed better able to function with the very small part of himself that he left behind to connect into the mesh of school life.

"Decline *jusjurandum*, Peasmarsh," Mr Fox, the Latin master, would say wearily, and Homer, like a zombie, never coming out of his abstraction, would mechanically recite the correct words.

"Give it a bit more *brio*, Peasmarsh," Mr Rendall, the English master, would snap as Homer read aloud a dozen lines from *Twelfth Night*, and Homer would obediently put a bit more expression in and raise his voice. It was as if he were able to switch on the autopilot.

On the whole, the masters left him alone; he gave the right answers in class, his homework was just adequate; they had more things to do than worry about a boy who seemed to be in a daze the whole time.

At games and sports, oddly enough, he even improved, just a little; his hand, raised in the air, would sometimes connect, as if accidentally, with the ball; he made a run, from time to time, in cricket; it really seemed that the less attention he paid to what he was doing, the more chance there was of his doing it successfully. He still had no friends and talked to nobody; all his spare time was spent in a corner of the library windowseat, or, in summer, sitting under one of the big lime trees by the side of the sports ground. A river ran just beyond them which bounded the school property; I wondered if it reminded him of the river at Downcombe. This was a different kind of river, though: deep and reedy and silent.

For a number of months, Homer and I exchanged hardly a word. Then, on my birthday (which comes in May) I found a little package in my locker. It was clumsily wrapped; the bulkiness of it reminded me, for some reason, of those parcels that Homer used to receive from his grandmother. I undid it with foreboding. And inside I discovered the little old copper whistle; I recognized it at once, and if I hadn't the initials would have reminded me.

Homer was nowhere about, but later I ran into him lurking in the cloakroom where we changed for sports. All the others had gone in to tea.

"Andrew," he said.

It was quite a shock to hear my first name. Of course we all used surnames at Watchetts.

"Well, what?"

"Did you get the whistle?"

"Yes I did. Thanks."

I felt awkward about it. I didn't want the whistle at all. What use was it to me? Besides, I felt that Homer was trying to buy his way back into my friendship, and I didn't want that either. Sparky and I were now friendly with another boy called Pango Swift, who played drums and guitar and was in the first eleven; and we were practising hard for the midsummer sports; in short, I had no time for Homer.

"It really isn't much use to me, Homer—er, Peasmarsh," I said. "Wouldn't you rather hang on to it? After all—" After all, I was going on to say, it's the only thing you've got left from the old days—but I suddenly remembered Homer's grandmother, with her shrewd tongue and her bright blue eyes, the brick floor of the cottage, the faded cotton chair covers, the grandfather clock, the taste of mushrooms and sausages and toasted home-made bread for supper; my voice for some reason died on me.

"No, I don't want it back," said Homer seriously. "I want you to do something for me."

Oh, oh. "Well, what?" I said again, very reluctantly.

"You see, I'm nearly able to get back there now."

"Get back? Get back *where?*"

The bell was ringing for tea, and it was raspberry-jam day; I could not feel much patience with Homer and his slow hesitant way of speaking. He was so dusty and shabby and fumbling; yet, in a way, with the straight pale hair, and his intent grey eyes and earnest manner, he seemed exactly the same as he had at seven.

"To Downcombe, of course," he said. "As I thought, it's all a technique of breathing control. You have to get out of synch. And then you can cross over to wherever you want. But what I'm not sure is, *how long can you stay?* Are you fixed at one point—or does time start to carry you forward again?"

"Have you gone absolutely bananas?" I said.

"Oh, do pay attention, Andrew. I've been reading an Indian scientist and philosopher called Swami Mansar Ray—a lot of what he says is just what old Holinshed believed. Only it's differently put, of course. Breathing control takes you out—like getting out of gear—and then, if you want to reconnect, a certain kind of sound will jolt you back to the time stratum you started from. Look, I'll show you; have you got the whistle?"

It was in my pocket. I produced it.

"Right; now, give me about three minutes and I'll show you."

"How do you mean, give you three minutes? Don't forget the tea-bell's gone."

"Three minutes before you blow the whistle, of course. Twist it right round. Then time me on your watch."

I could see his breathing become slower and slower. Presently it seemed to stop entirely.

"Homer, are you all right? Homer! Answer me!"

"The volume of a given mass of gas varies inversely with the pressure, provided the temperature remains constant,"

127

he replied in a calm, mechanical voice. "Thank you, Wilson, I am perfectly all right."

I wasn't at all certain of this; also, I wanted my tea; so after two minutes, not three, I blew the soundless whistle and was relieved to see a touch of red come back into Homer's wax-coloured cheeks and his breathing begin to deepen.

Then for the first time I noticed that in his hand he was holding a parti-coloured knitted pot-holder.

"You didn't give me enough time," he said reproachfully. "*Three* minutes was what I told you, not two. I only just had time to grab this."

"Where the dickens did that come from?"

"Don't you recognize it?"

I did, as a matter of fact; his grandmother used to make them and always had a couple hanging on a hook beside the kitchen oil-stove.

"Why in the world do you carry that about?"

"I just brought it from *there*."

"I—oh, look here, that's rubbish! I don't believe you. I'm going to tea, see you later."

But just the same I did feel almost shaken; the pot-holder was so very familiar. But still . . . Well, I didn't want to think about it.

Homer grabbed my arm, though, as I was about to leave him.

"Andrew—listen. You said you'd do something for me."

I had not, but I found it hard to drag myself rudely from his clutch.

"If you see me—well, *gone*, like that, for a really long time—more than an hour, say—will you blow the whistle and get me back? Just in case—well, in case there proves to be a catch in it somewhere? It's marvellous, but I still have a lot to learn—haven't quite got the hang—"

"I can't keep an eye on you all the time," I said crossly. "How am I supposed to do that? Have a bit of sense!"

"Just the same—please do, Andrew?"

"Oh, all right."

I wondered if I ought to say something about him to Matron, or his form master. My promise was pretty useless, really, for we weren't in the same stream now.

Still, once in a while we found ourselves in a class together. One of these was carpentry, at which Homer had been unremarkably bad; he was clumsy with tools and not at all interested; he dropped things, spoiled wood, it took him weeks to learn to make a simple joint. But now, I noticed that in a state of dreamy calm he was completing a very neat mortice with slots in a table leg and corresponding tongues of wood on the two side-pieces. All his attention was elsewhere, far away; perhaps at Downcombe. Sliding the whistle out of my pocket I surreptitiously turned facing the wall and blew a soundless blast.

Homer jerked, and cut his finger with the chisel, and said something sharp under his breath. Five minutes later, passing my bench, he whispered reproachfully, "Why did you have to blow it just *then*? I hadn't been gone long! It was a wonderful hot blowy July day, and we'd been picking wild strawberries all afternoon, and Granny was going to make jam."

"Was I there too?"

"Of course. And much nicer then. I wish you hadn't blown—"

"Well you asked me," I said crossly.

"I know I did." He had the grace to look apologetic. "Thanks, anyway, I daresay it's a good thing to come back and check up."

The next time I blew for Homer was after a church service one Sunday. I'd noticed him utterly rapt in a corner of a pew. That time he gave me a somewhat startled nod and blink, and muttered to me after a moment,

"I'd been there for about six weeks . . ."

"What was that poor dumb jerk talking to you about?" inquired Sparky, strolling up behind us and thumping my head with a prayer book as Homer shambled out of the chapel.

"Oh," I said reluctantly, "just a kind of nutty idea that he has."

"What about?"

"Going back into the past." We were walking back towards the main school buildings. I hoped Sparky would abandon the subject.

"Going back into the past? But how *sublime*," said Sparky. Sublime was his word just then.

It was a fine hot morning and we were going to do some sports training. "Tell me more," Sparky said, as we changed into running shoes. "How does our Peasmarsh set about it?"

"By—by a kind of breathing control. And then—then, the theory is that a particular kind of sound jerks him back into the present time again."

"Why, this is quite riveting," said Sparky as we strolled out towards the sports ground. "Do, please, continue. *What* particular kind of sound?"

Feeling that I shouldn't, I fished out the whistle from the pocket of my running-shorts. "When I blow this."

Sparky studied the small copper tube attentively and asked its history; I told him what I knew about it.

"Are you ready?" bawled Enthoven, the sports master. "First group for the hundred yards sprint: on your marks, get set—GO!"

We were in the second group, so Sparky continued to study the whistle.

130

"You say," he pondered, "that our dear friend Peasmarsh is *happy* in the past; happier than he is at this delightful educational establishment?"

"Well—yes—I suppose that's where he really—"

"Second group!" yelled Enthoven. I hurriedly grabbed the whistle back from Sparky; we crouched, got set, then ran as if the Devil were at our heels. Sparky beat me by a tenth of a second.

"Then," he went on as if nothing had happened; his breathing control was almost as good as Homer's, "would it not be better for all concerned if our mutual friend were to *stay* in the past? Let's see that whistle again."

Slowly I handed it to him. We were now at the far end of the sports ground, under the lime trees. Sparky calmly tossed the whistle so that it flew in a wide, glittering arc and landed in the river, where it made no more splash than a minnow rising.

"Third group!" bawled Mr Enthoven. "On your marks, get set—"

Homer was in the third group. Normally he was an undistinguished runner, generally arriving last, well after all the others; but on this occasion he amazed everybody by drawing effortlessly to the front of the group, then far, far ahead; his speed must have been about double that of anybody else who ran that afternoon.

"WELL DONE, Peasmarsh!" yelled the sports master.

But Homer did not stop running when he passed the tape; he kept right on, faster and faster, straight into the river, and disappeared from view.

Nor did he come up again; the Yarrow runs very fast. When his body was at last discovered, it had been washed about a mile downstream.

*

131

I worry about Homer a great deal. I wake in the night, sweating and trembling; I imagine him, alone in that cottage, with no gas, no electricity, only candles; with Rusty, the old spaniel who died when we were eight. Sometimes I think I can hear Rusty howl; sometimes I think I can hear the brown wall of water rolling down the valley, smashing banks, knocking trees aside, hoisting up rocks, pouring over the meadows, coming to overwhelm the little house.

The Blades

Right from the start they were enemies. Or at least on opposite sides. Maybe that was to be expected with two boys so diametrically different from each other as Jack Kettering and Will Donkine. Kettering was tall, or tallish, solidly built, with a flat, high-cheekboned, ruddy, handsome face, and a thick crop of burnished red-gold hair. His dad was a Master of Foxhounds, and when the older Kettering came to the school for speech days you could see just what Jack would become in the course of time—solid, swaggering, red-faced, with his thatch of shining hair turned snowy white. Kettering excelled at all sports—cricket, football, rowing, swimming, athletics; and he was by no means a fool, either; he had a knack of learning anything by heart that could be learned in that way, so grammar, mathematical and scientific formulae, dates and facts were always at his fingers' ends—passing exams was no trouble to him, he was generally among the top four or five at the year's end. He could be funny, too, in a rather unsubtle way, and generous—at least to his friends—he had that sort of air about him which people like Francis Drake and Robin Hood must have carried, so that followers, as it were, flocked to his standard. Not that I mean to say he was an outlaw—oh dear, no. Law-abiding, on the whole, was Jack, more so as he went up the school; of course there was the odd quiet escapade—beer drunk behind the Art studios and then whisky in the boathouse, dodging off to go to the Motor Show and a night on the spree in London—but these were just schoolboy capers, nothing nasty about them. He enjoyed the reputation of being a good-natured, easy-going fellow. His lot (there were about half a dozen of them, the Blades, they called themselves) were the same kind, and they stuck together all the way up the school. Later on, when girls were admitted into the upper forms, they all acquired girlfriends to match: Kettering's girl was called Pamela Cassell, and she was big and blooming and bossy, with a head of brick-red hair to match Jack's copper-gold, always freshly shampooed, shining and crisp. Captain of the girls' hockey, she was, won the tennis cup three years running, and intended to run a ballroom-dancing school. She had that pink-and-white complexion often found in redheads, and pale china-blue eyes; striking, people said she was, but I couldn't see it myself. If you didn't belong to Kettering's group her eyes passed over you in utter rejection, you might as well have been a garden bench.

Donkine, Will Donkine was, as I've said, in all ways the complete opposite of Jack. From the start, poor devil, he suffered from his name. Will was short for Willibald, which was a family name; some ancestor had come from Austria— Willibald Edvard Donkine, his full name was, so if he wasn't called the Hun, or Kraut, or Donk, or Donkey, it was Weed or Weedy because of his initials. He came to the school when he was twelve, and by the time he was fourteen the various nicknames had more or less settled down into Donk. Of course it cut no ice at all that his father, Sir Joel Donkine, was a well-known scientist, in line for the Nobel Prize. Will Donkine was small and bony, with a pale, hollow-eyed face, short-sighted serious dark-brown eyes (he had to wear steel-rimmed glasses which were always getting broken), and sparse no-colour hair like a crop of mousy moss on top of his undistinguished head. Being so shortsighted he was no use at games, and anyway his arms and legs were thin as sticks of celery so he couldn't run fast or catch balls or hit them; he was bright enough, but his wits had a habit of wandering, so that he didn't do particularly well in exams; when he ought to have been answering Question Two, he'd be looking out of the window trying to estimate the flight-speed of swifts, or wondering if it would be possible to turn a Black Hole inside out, or to compress Mars Bars to the size of dice for rapid and economic distribution. His conversation was always interesting —he knew a lot about codes, and ESP, and how people's discarded selves may come back to haunt them (he read books on psychology when most people were reading *Biggles*) and where you can still find bits of primeval forest in Europe, and what to do if you sit on a queen bee, but his knowledge wasn't very well applied; it never turned up when it was needed. I liked Donkine's company, but he wasn't a popular boy. Part of that was his own fault. He found most people boring; simply preferred his own thoughts. I expect they were more interesting than locker-room chat, but, just the same, if you don't want to have a dismal time at school you need to meet people half-way, display a bit of give-and-take. Donkine did nothing of that kind, so he was an outcast. His solitary state didn't worry him in the least, he spent his spare time reading in the library or measuring things in the lab, or working in his allotment. He was very keen on gardening.

It must be said that Kettering and the Blades gave him a fairly hard time, specially when we were all younger; every now and then they'd rough him up, not *too* much, of course, because they didn't want to spoil their reputation for being decent types; never anything that would show. To do Donkine justice, he never grassed on them; for a day or two he'd go about rather more silent and hunched over, shabbier and a trifle more moth-eaten looking, that was all. What he did mind was when they messed up his garden; that really hit him in a tender spot. But, as luck would have it, old Postlethwaite the science master was out at three a.m. one night studying a comet and came on Kettering and McGeech systematically digging up Will's artichokes and celeriac, so there was a certain amount of fuss about that, and from then on they had to lay off the garden sabotage; it would have been too obvious that it was them, see? They had to think of other forms of persecution.

While Kettering and the Blades were acquiring girlfriends and boasting of their exploits, Will made friends with my sister, Ceridwen, who was small and dark and cross-looking. Nothing romantic about their friendship: they were both interested in the same kinds of things. Ceridwen intended to do animal and plant breeding later on, and she was very impressed with Will's aptitude for growing things.

By the time we were in the lower fifth, Will's father had invented his dust extractor, D.R.I.P., it was called, Dust Removal from Industrial and Institutional Premises, but of course it was shortened to DRIP. Don't ask me how it worked—it was a thermo-nuclear process, radioactivity came into it, and magnetic fields, and the earth's rotation and gravitational pull. Unlike many such processes, it was simple and economical to instal. What it did was suck all the dust and grit and germs out of the air inside a building by means of vents on the floor, so that once a DRIP System was installed in your factory—or office block—or hospital—you need never sweep or dust or Hoover or scrub again. There have been similar systems in the past, of course, but expensive to run, and none were so efficient as Sir J. Donkine's. Apparently it really did remove every particle and molecule of anything nasty from the atmosphere, so that the air you breathed into your lungs was 100% Simon pure.

Naturally a process, an invention like this was nothing like so sensational as discovering penicillin or DNA or splitting the atom; but still there were articles about it in scientific journals, and old Corfe, our headmaster, mentioned it in a congratulatory way one morning at Assembly, and said we must all be proud that Sir J was an Old Boy of our school and his son was our dear fellow-scholar, and we must hope that Will would invent something equally useful one day. I noticed Will give a kind of blink behind his glasses at that; he was not at all gratified by being singled out, and I knew why; of course for him it would mean extra hazing and sarcastic broadsides from the Blades for several weeks, till the news had settled down. Old Corfe, who never knew anything about what went on in the school, was unaware of that; and he was pleased as a dog with two tails about the publicity for the school.

Because of this connection—and before anyone had finished asking What About Side Effects—our school, along with several hospitals and a Midland furniture factory, had taken the plunge and had the Donkine DRIP System installed. A demonstration of loyalty it was, on our part, to show our faith and pride in our Old Boy (though I bet that Mr Corfe managed to get the installation done at half-price because of the public interest etc., etc.). Anyway, air vents were set into the floors of all rooms, in corners where they were not inconvenient, and suction pipes, and a big gleaming white tank down in the basement which housed the works. If you held your breath and nobody else was breathing in the room you could just catch the sound of a very faint hum, no more noise than a lightbulb makes when it's at the point of death. Nobody could say the DRIP System was loud or annoying. And the school certainly was clean! Not a speck of

mud, no dust or fluff could lie on any surface for more than a
moment, our clothes and books and bedding and towels all
stayed cleaner longer, even substances like spilled jam or glue
tended to vanish overnight if not wiped up; and at the end of
the first term old Corfe announced with triumph that our
health rate had improved by eighty per cent, practically no
head colds, hay fever, or asthma, and all other infectious
complaints much reduced.

The hospitals and furniture factory had reported the same
good results; by now Sir Joel Donkine was on the highroad to
success, fame, fortune, and the Nobel Prize. DripCo, the
company formed to make the DRIP Systems, could hardly
keep pace with the orders; every factory and hospital in the
country wanted them now; they were being installed not only
in public buildings but also in private homes. Buckingham
Palace, if you can call that a private home, was first on the list,
and Sir Joel got a decoration from the Palace as well as his
Nobel.

What was his son Will doing all this time? Will, of course,
had known about his father's intentions long ago, heard the
subject discussed since he was nine or ten. His mother had
died, when he was six, of an anti-immunity failure, so Sir Joel
tended to talk to him a lot when they were together; one
reason why Will found most school conversation boring.

Will's main problem after Sir Joel's rise to fame was
dodging retribution from the Society of Blades—what they
called 'necessary discipline' to stop him from getting above
himself. *Above himself*—poor Will sometimes looked as if he
wished he was under the ground. Most of the Blades, by now,
were big and tough as grown men, whereas Will, at fifteen,
seemed to have stopped growing for good and was no bigger
than a thirteen-year-old. It wasn't for lack of fresh air; he still
spent hours every day tending his garden. Unfortunately the

school allotments were isolated beyond a row of utility sheds, on the edge of the school grounds; he was much at risk there from the attentions of the Blades.

"How's our little Drip today, how's our Weed?" they would say, clustering round him affectionately. "We've come to remind you not to get too stuck up, just because your dad invented a giant Hoover."

Once they painted him all over with Stockholm tar, which he'd been using on a peach tree he grew from a peach-stone; another time they dropped him, and all his tools, into the river; on a third occasion they removed tufts of hair from all over his head. The effect was a bit like a chessboard. That was a mistake, because it was quite visible; old Corfe made inquiries, sent for Kettering and the Blades, and gave them a severe tongue-lashing and various penalties, so their attentions abated for a while.

And Donkine went doggedly on his way, reading a lot, keeping up reasonably well with school work, showing fitful brilliance here and there, specially in Chemistry and Biology; working in his garden and trying to mind his own business. Whatever that was.

"Don't you ever want to get your own back on those pigs?" my sister, Ceridwen, asked him once. We are Welsh; I reckon revenge comes more naturally to us. But Will just shrugged.

"What's the point?" he said. "They'd only make it worse for me, after. You've got to think ahead. And I've got better things to do than conduct a feud. Besides, I have an idea that by and by . . ."

He didn't finish his sentence. His eyes had wandered, as they often did, towards two huge shiny pink potatoes he had just dug up, and a tussock of grass he had pulled out.

One thing he had discovered was that DRIP compost was marvellous for the garden.

I expect you have been wondering what happened to all the dirt and dust that was sucked out of the classrooms and offices and dormitories. It went into black plastic sacks that fitted over the outlet-vents and were removed at regular intervals. The stuff inside them was like stiff dark-brown prune jam, very thick and sticky. Will found that if this was diluted and watered on to the garden, or just spaded around in gooey lumps like undercooked Christmas pudding, it worked wonders for growing plants. A few weeks of this treatment and Will's artichokes were big as footballs, his spinach-leaves the size of the *Daily Mirror*, and his roses six inches in diameter.

Postlethwaite the science master (we called him Old Possum, of course, because he had big, wide-apart gentle eyes, and very little chin, and his thin hair wavered backwards like water-weeds), old Postlethwaite was absolutely delighted at this link-up between the activities of father and son, evidence of Will's independent research.

"Wonderful work, wonderful, my dear Donkine," he kept saying. "You may have hit on something of real importance there." And he quoted: " 'Whoever could make two blades of grass grow where only one grew before, would deserve better of mankind than the whole race of politicians put together.' Do you know who said that?"

"Swift," said Will without hesitation. But his mind as usual seemed half astray. "People wore wigs in Swift's day, didn't they, sir?"

"We must see if we can't get you the Wickenden Award for this," Old Possum went on.

The Wickenden Cup was a school honour endowed by a past rich American parent; it was given from time to time for unusually original school work.

"Oh, *please*, sir, don't bother," said Will, who knew that

anything of the kind would only lead to more trouble with Kettering's group. "If you could just ask Mr Corfe to give an order that the black sacks aren't to be taken away by the garbage trucks but left in a heap here by the allotments. Then everybody who wants to can use them."

But nobody else took the trouble to do so. It's true the stuff did smell rather vile: sweet and rotten, like malt and codliver oil.

By and by there began to be odd, apparently disconnected paragraphs in the newspapers: the Queen had been obliged to cancel all her engagements, as she was suffering from a virus cold; a hospital in the North was plagued by an epidemic of ringworm or possibly infectious alopecia; the staff of a Midland furniture factory were all out on strike for some mysterious reason; and the Prime Minister, in the middle of a visit to Moscow, returned to Britain hurriedly and unexpectedly.

Could there be a link between these incidents? The factory and the hospital were two which had been among the first to have the DRIP System installed.

At our school, though, we didn't read the papers a lot; interested in our own affairs, we weren't much concerned with outside news. Time had skidded on its way and by now we were working for our O levels, up to the eyes in reading and revision. Still, even busy as we were, we couldn't help observing something that was happening right under our noses.

Ceridwen, my sharp-eyed sister, spotted it first.

"All the staff are going bald. Have you noticed?" she said.

It was true. The men's hair was receding at a rapid rate, and the women teachers had taken to various ruses—buns, chignons, hair-pieces—to try to conceal the fact that their locks were becoming scantier and scantier. It seemed to affect older people faster.

Then one morning there was a crisis in the girls' dormitory.

Hysterical shrieks were heard coming from the room of big redheaded Pamela Cassell (who by this time was a prefect and so entitled to a room of her own); she had locked herself in and refused to come out. When Mrs Budleigh, the matron, finally opened up with a master-key, it was said that she let out almost as loud a squawk as the frantic girl inside. For—Ceridwen told me and Will, then the news spread like lightning through the girls' dorm and so out and about the main school—all Pam Cassell's thick glossy red hair, of which she had been so proud that she let it grow to waist length—all that hair had fallen out in the night and the wretched girl was now bald as an egg, while the hair lay in a tangled mess on her pillow.

Well! What a thing! Needless to say, Pamela was whisked away to a skin and hair specialist; and what he said was so unhelpful that she flatly refused to come back to school, as long as she was such a spectacle, so that was the last we saw of her. Will certainly wasn't sorry. In the old days she used sometimes to stand by and watch while the Blades did things to him.

Meanwhile the mysterious doom struck again: several other people became bald overnight in the same manner, while the hair of others began falling out at a frightening rate. Fair people were much worse affected than dark; I remember watching a blond boy called Titheredge combing his hair one day in the cloakroom, and it was like watching a Flymo go through a patch of hay—three quarters of the hair came away with the comb.

Jack Kettering's was a spectacular case. People from different forms read out the notices each day after Assembly. Tuesday it's the fifth formers. Kettering did it one Tuesday, he had a nervous habit, on public occasions, of brushing his hair back with his left hand, and when he did it this time the entire thick reddish-fair thatch fell right off on to the floor behind him. The whole school gasped in horrified amusement and then—reaction, I suppose—a roar of laughter went up. People were rocking from side to side, falling about—how could they help it? The startled Kettering ran his hands over his smooth bare scalp, glanced in appalled disbelief at the heap of hair on the floor behind him, then turned white as a rag and bolted from the school hall.

I noticed that Will Donkine was looking very thoughtful.

"Did *you* do that?" Ceridwen asked him, after Assembly was over. "I mean—did you make his hair fall out?"

Both of us had a lot of respect for Donkine; we could quite believe that he was capable of it.

But . . . "No," he answered slowly. "No, I had nothing to do with it. Though I'm not surprised—I had an idea something like that was due. And I can't say I'm sorry—when I remember some of the things those big bullies did to me."

He gave a reminiscent rub to his own meagre mouse-brown thatch—which, like everyone else's, was getting noticeably thinner. Ceridwen and I have black hair. It took longer than anybody's to go, but it went in the end.

"No; I didn't do it," Will said. "But I expect I'll be in trouble from Kettering's lot soon enough, if what I think is true."

"What's that?"

"Why, it must be an effect of my father's dust extractor, don't you see? The Queen hasn't been out for ages—they had one in Buck House. And the PM had one at Ten Downing Street—and I'm sure she's been wearing a wig for weeks. Have you noticed the newspaper photographs? And then there's that hospital, and the Biffin factory—it'll be all over the country soon, I expect. Father's always a bit too hasty . . ."

Of course events have proved Will right. A few months more, and all the buildings which had installed DRIP Systems were populated by totally bald inhabitants.

In three weeks our school, which of course was among the first innovators, couldn't show a single hair among the six hundred students and the forty staff. Even Smokey, the school cat, had gone bald as a pig, and was rechristened Pinky. Even the mice, when seen, could be seen to be bald. Punk cuts, crew cuts, Afro heads, Rastafarian plaits, beehives, all had vanished, like snow-wreaths in thaw, as the poet says.

In a way, our all being companions in misfortune made the state easier to bear. I found it interesting to notice how school relationships and pecking orders had changed and reversed, now that our appearance was so different. At first we found it quite difficult to recognize one another; with no hair, just pale bald scalps, we all looked alike, you couldn't tell boys from girls, we seemed like members of some Eastern sect, ready to bang gongs or spin prayer-wheels; and the people who hitherto had prided themselves on their looks went round as humbly as anybody else.

Meanwhile there was a terrific public outcry and fuss. After a while, as Will had predicted, somebody put two and two together and traced the baldness to the Donkine DRIP system. Most of the purchasers of DRIP Systems thereupon switched them off, hoping that the hair of employees, patients, students and nurses would begin to grow again. But it didn't. Some vital growing hormone, it seemed, had been sucked out for good; or at least, for a generation.

About this time Sir Joel Donkine came back to England from the Brazilian forests, where he had been on a research expedition. Naturally he was aghast at what had happened and made a statement about it.

"I accept full blame and responsibility," he said to the

newspapers, before his lawyers could warn him not to, and in no time lawsuits and writs amounting to God knows how many millions were piling upon his doorstep.

"Dad's so impetuous," Will said again thoughtfully. "He sounds off without checking the probabilities."

I thought how different his son was. But perhaps I was wrong.

People said Sir Joel ought to have his Nobel and CBE taken away. He was probably the most unpopular man in Europe —though his System had prevented hundreds of colds and other infections? All that was forgotten in the wave of fury. People marched with placards demanding Give Us Back Our Hair!

Unisex shops and barbers and the manufacturers of shampoos, conditioners, setting lotions, hairbrushes, combs, hairgrips, clasps, nets, ribbons, bathing caps, dyes, tints and bleaches were all after Sir Joel's blood.

Taken away their livelihood he had, see?

Nobody thought to mention that, on the other side of the scale, makers of wigs, hairpieces, headsquares, hats, caps, hoods, and bonnets were doing a roaring trade. Tattoo artists stencilled ingenious hair designs over people's naked heads, or just drew pretty patterns; colourful head paint was invented; at least part of the population remembered that the Ancient Egytians went bald from choice, and discovered that there were quite a few conveniences about the bald state.

But as an unusually hot summer drew on there were a few cases of sunstroke, and questions were asked in Parliament, and people began to say that Sir J. Donkine should be impeached, or hung, drawn and quartered, or at least tried for causing grievous public harm.

An inquiry was proposed. But before its machinery could be set up—public inquiries are very slow-moving things—

poor Sir Joel was dead. Heart failure, the Coroner's report announced. And I daresay that was correct. I'm pretty sure that he had died of a broken heart.

"Poor Father," Will said sadly. "All he wanted was to help people. He wanted to prevent their getting infections like the one that killed Mother. And so he landed himself in all this trouble. He never would think before he acted."

Will grieved very much for his father—the more so as he had no other relations and would now have to become a Ward of Court.

After Sir Joel's death, Kettering's group had the grace to leave Will alone for a while; nobody these days had the spirit for recriminations. Also we were all working like Stakhanovites for our O levels . . .

Will's results in those were fairly remarkable, considering all he had been through. He came top of our lot, way ahead of anybody else. And when we re-assembled in the autumn term he seemed in reasonably good shape. He had spent the summer with Mr Postlethwaite; the Old Possum had offered to put him up so he wouldn't have to go into Care. And apparently he had passed most of the holidays in biological research.

"Boy's got a really amazing mind," I heard the Old Possum one day tell Mrs Budleigh in the cafeteria. "Kind of results he's getting wouldn't disgrace those fellows in the Bickerden Labs at Cambridge. What he's working after, I do believe, is to make up for the harm his father did—or felt he had done, poor man."

"The harm he did seems quite real enough to me," replied the matron coldly, adjusting her wig. "If the boy thinks he can discover some way of making people's hair grow again, I consider that a very proper ambition."

Will was wholly uncommunicative about his work. Most of

it was carried out in the labs—he didn't have time for gardening these days—and it required buckets and buckets of the DRIP System compost which was still piled in black shiny sackfuls by the side of the allotments. He fiddled about with test tubes and cultures and filters, he painted black and brown grease on to mushrooms, and eggs, and frogs, and the bald school mice, and guinea pigs. Ceridwen helped him.

By and by he began to look more hopeful; a spark came back into his eye that had been missing for many months; and strangely enough he began to grow, quite suddenly shot up so tall and lanky that he overtopped Kettering and most of the Blades. By now that group had rather fallen apart; two or three of the Blades had left school after their undistinguished O Levels; Pamela, of course, departed after the loss of her hair, and Jack Kettering himself was fairly subdued these days. Becoming bald had changed him a lot. Whereas Will's hair was such a modest crop and unremarkable colour that its going made little difference to his looks—indeed, thin-faced, with dark, deepset eyes and newly acquired horn-rimmed glasses he now seemed quite impressive—Jack Kettering without any hair looked flat-faced, florid, and stupid, somewhere between a pig and a seal. And was nothing like so aggressive as he used to be.

Indeed I noticed that nowadays he was cautiously friendly and almost obsequious towards Will, went out of his way to address remarks to him, pass the sugar for his cereal at breakfast, and so forth. Will didn't take much notice, just went on his own way as usual.

One day he captured Pinky the cat (no problem, they had been friends for years) and bore him off to the lab. When next seen, Pinky's pale uncatlike exterior had been dyed all over a delicate rust brown.

"You think the Animal Protection League would approve of what you've done to that poor dumb animal?" demanded Mrs Budleigh, fixing Will with a sharp grey eye.

"Sure they would; it was done for his own good," Will answered positively. "But, if you think it would be better, I'll fix him up with an insulation jacket while I wait for results." And Ceridwen helped him construct the cat a butter-muslin jacket, which was sewn up his back so he couldn't get it off. (Pinky showed no gratitude; Ceridwen's hands were quite badly scratched.)

The cat's head was left uncovered and, after a week, anybody gently rubbing under his chin or above his eyes could feel a faint stubble of something growing. This caused a sensation, as you can imagine; people rushed to Will to offer themselves as guinea pigs for his treatment.

Old Corfe, the headmaster, was down on this.

"Donkine is working hard and I'm sure all our good wishes are with him, but I think it wholly inadvisable that any of the rest of you should submit yourselves as research material, at least without parental consent. We know by now—alas!— what disastrous effects the best intentioned work may produce."

Anyway it seemed that Will didn't want guinea pigs; he turned away all the people who tapped at the lab door and offered their bald heads for his process.

All but one.

"I've got Dad's consent!" Jack Kettering told him in an urgent whisper. "I phoned home and asked him. He says I look so Godawful now that anything would be better. Come on, now, Donk—be a sport! I know I've laughed at you a bit in the past, in a friendly way, but that's all over long ago—isn't it? We're good friends now, aren't we?"

He looked up beseechingly into Will's face. Will said. "You

realize it may not be just ordinary hair that grows back?"

"Anything, horsehair, sheep's wool, would be better than having a dome like an egg. I don't care *what* it is, just *do* it, old fellar."

So Donkine painted Jack's scalp a rusty brown, and Ceridwen stitched him a butter-muslin skull-cap to cover the painted area.

"What's that for?"

"To stop birds pecking it," replied Will gravely.

"*Birds?*"

"Or anything else. You never know. Wear the cap till I tell you."

Two weeks passed. Pinky the cat's muslin jacket seemed to be getting tight; perhaps he was growing.

One evening, as we all sat at supper, Pinky hurtled in through the open dining room window carrying a struggling, cheeping sparrow. The cat had torn his jacket in the chase, it flapped loose, and one of the girls, rushing to the rescue of the sparrow, let out a quack of amazement.

"The cat's gone green!"

"Take off the remains of the jacket," suggested old Postlethwaite.

Ceridwen pulled it off, tearing the tattered muslin with no trouble—to reveal Pinky, erstwhile Smokey, wearing a fine coat of short velvety green.

Someone said in an awed voice, "That cat is covered with *grass.*"

"May I be utterly blessed!" muttered Old Possum. He gazed with bulging eyes at the verdant animal. Will poured the cat a saucer of milk and inspected him with serious satisfaction as he drank.

"It worked with the mice, and it seems to have worked with him. I found it impossible, you see, sir, to grow hair on anything

—but grass responded very well—and, after all, it makes just as good a cover . . ."

Jack Kettering, who had come in late for tea, arrived in time to hear this remark. Without a word, he spun on his heel and strode back into the hall, where there is a big wall mirror, dragging off his muslin cap as he went. We heard him let out a kind of astonished wail.

"*Grass. . . !*"

Will strolled out after him, and I could hear him say mildly, "You did tell me that anything would be better than having a dome like an egg—"

"I didn't bargain on *grass!*"

But by that time half the school were frothing around Will, clamouring and begging: "Do me, do me, do *me*! I'd *like* grass! Maybe there could be a few buttercups as well? Or a daisy?"

"I shan't do anybody without parental permission," Will said gravely.

I saw him glance, over the clustered shining bald heads, towards Old Possum, with a kind of rueful resigned shrug and gesture of the head. Postlethwaite's expression was still fairly stunned.

"After all, sir," Will went on in a reasonable tone, "you did say that to make two blades of grass grow where one grew before was a good thing to do. And I've made two blades grow where *none* grew before. Think what a hay crop we'd get, off the heads of everyone here."

But I could imagine what Old Possum was thinking, for I was thinking it myself. After grass has been established for a while, you get larger plants rooting, and then larger ones still, and then acorns which sprout into oak trees . . .

Will was just as impulsive as his father. And who is going to deal with the next lot of side effects?

Aunt Susan

All their friends said, and thought as well, that the young Caraways were a delightful couple: simple, unpretentious, easy to please, fond of all kinds of fun, happy in their uncomplicated lives. Not intellectual, not snobbish, not avant-garde, not reactionary—there was really nothing at all wrong with the Caraways. They lived in a charming Queen Anne cottage on the edge of Pinchester, a delightful country town; Delia taught in the local primary school, but the pair had not been married very long, and everyone felt it was only a matter of time before a few even younger Caraways were born, and then Delia, so home-loving, so maternal, so natural, would certainly give up her job and devote herself to her children.

Simon Caraway had been an insurance agent, and quite good at it, but just for fun he had written a thriller and shown it to a friend who had connections with a publishing house; the manuscript was read, approved, published, and did most creditabiy; so now Simon found himself launched on a comfortable and lucrative career producing a suspense novel every nine months. To friends who exclaimed in amazement, "Where *do* you get your ideas? How in the world do you think up those awful plots in such a peaceful little spot as Pinchester?" he pointed out that all he required to do was to read the national and local press every day, where headlines such as 'Amusement Park "Dummy" Proves to be Corpse of Shot Man', 'Ex-Teacher Jailed for Drug-running', 'Gypsy Curse Worries Local Council', 'Robot Runs Amok in Lab, Kills Five', 'Widower Instals Closed-circuit Line to Wife's Tomb', and 'Wife Succeeds at Fifth Attempt to Poison Husband' kept him amply supplied with ideas for plots.

So, year after year, Simon's books continued to appear in their black-and-honey-coloured jackets; 'the new Simon Caraway' was always in demand at every library, and, although not affluent, the couple lived very comfortably, since their tastes were far from expensive. Delia did all the housework and cooking herself; Simon grew, in their half acre of garden, nearly all the vegetables they consumed, for he made a practice of writing only in the morning hours, devoting afternoons to exercise, and so keeping his health and youthful appearance.

Life went on with them pleasantly and tranquilly until the death of Uncle Paul Palliser. Paul and Susan Palliser had taken care of Delia when she was a child, her own parents having perished in a motor accident, so it was natural for her to say to Simon:

"Poor, dear, Aunt Susan, I can't bear to think of her living alone, she's such a sociable person. Would you mind terribly, Simon, if I invited her to come and live with us? There *is* the whole top floor."

There was. For the expected little Caraways had, somehow, never materialized. Delia and Simon kept meaning to convert the space to a self-contained flat, and rent it to a teacher or student from the local college of education; but somehow they had never got round to the operation.

It was equally natural for good-natured Simon to reply, "Poor old Aunt Susan, she must be feeling terribly at a loose end. She used to do everything for old Paul. Of course, darling, go ahead and invite her if you want to. Heaven knows there's room for a whole army of aunts up on the top floor."

So Aunt Susan was invited; and piled all her worldly goods into a pantechnicon, and came; and within a fortnight was so settled into the life of Pinchester that it was hard to remember she had not always been there. She was exceedingly fond of the young couple downstairs, and touchingly anxious to make herself useful to them; she offered to cat-sit (since there was no baby); she offered to help with the housework, she offered to share in the gardening, she wanted to be a functioning member of the household in every possible way; the only hindrance to this was that the young Caraways were so self-sufficient already. However Aunt Susan had her own resources; she made petit-point and she was a corresponding member of several Psychological Societies, and found some local clubs of a similar nature to join; she attended lectures, gave them herself, and seemed happy and occupied enough.

But after a while Simon Caraway, though he would not dream of finding fault with his wife's aunt, who was as well-meaning as she could possibly be, could find it in his heart just the same to wish that she would not explain his own mental processes to him quite so often. If he broke the handle off a cup she would say, "Ah, that was a protest, because Delia set a small teacup for you and you subconsciously wanted a *large* cup of tea." If he bruised himself chopping kindling, or pulled a muscle while digging, or suffered one of the other minor injuries to which all gardeners are liable, she would say, "Aha! That's because you wanted a pretext for not coming to the town council meeting with Delia and me, but wanted to stay comfortably at home and watch the Western on TV." If he forgot something, she could always supply a reason for his absentmindedness, generally a discreditable one; and if he employed logic in countering her suggestions, she said that his logic only masked and rationalized some deep-down un-acknowledged atavistic motive.

Simon bore with all this good-temperedly enough, until Aunt Susan started in on his thrillers. She had not read any of them before coming to live with her niece; she was not in the habit of reading much fiction at all, and certainly none in the blood-and-thunder genre; but she was a conscientious and well-mannered person; she felt that, since she was now living under his roof, it was incumbent upon her to make herself familiar with her nephew-in-law's work, so she purchased half a dozen of his paperbacks, took them to bed with her one night, and worked her way doggedly through them.

Since she had read nothing of this nature before they had an extremely drastic effect on her; from that day she regarded Simon with a new eye.

"I'm afraid, Simon dear, that you have some terribly deep unresolved conflicts inside you," was her inaugural statement.

"I'm quite sure you're wrong, Aunt Susan," he blithely replied. "Or, if I have, my subconscious has managed to keep them awfully well concealed from me up till now. I'm really very happy and satisfied with my life, you know! I love Delia, I love this house and town, I love the garden, I make a good living—I haven't a care in the world."

"If only you could get at that subterranean layer of turbulence," she sighed. "Really it's *terrifying*—the evidence of it is so apparent in your writing."

"So," he pointed out, "aren't I lucky? For it's extremely lucrative. *The Curse on Clapham Common* has just sold to an American book club for thirty thousand dollars, and *The Deadly Dummy* is going into a third printing, and they are negotiating for film rights of *Telex to the Tomb*."

"I'm afraid you don't have any conception of just how serious, how terribly dangerous this may be. I *wish* you would go to an analyst, Simon—just to indulge me, just to set my mind at rest."

"But, dear Aunt, just suppose he analysed all my deep subconscious conflicts out of me—then how would I earn a living? I don't suppose that I'd be able to get back into the insurance business now—and I'd hate to have to live on Delia's earnings."

"Well," sighed Aunt Susan, "perhaps if you did something *really* creative for at least part of the time—for you can hardly say that writing those bloodcurdling little books is a suitable activity for a full-grown, adult human being—and if you were to give up writing—even for a few months—that might straighten you out and make a tremendous difference."

"Well," he said thoughtfully, "I daresay I *could* leave off writing for a few months—*The Curse* is doing uncommonly well—and a few months without earning might make a useful tax-loss—but what kind of creative activity did you have in mind, Aunt Susan?"

Handweaving was what Aunt Susan had in mind, it appeared; in no time at all she had a large loom installed in the dining room, all the furniture was squeezed into one corner, and Simon was receiving instruction from one of Aunt Susan's new acquaintances, a neighbouring lady who was a weaving enthusiast; and so, for several months, each day after breakfast, instead of going to rattle away at the typewriter in his study, Simon would go to what was now known as the loom room, and the clonk and thud of the shuttle could be heard and sometimes Simon's muttered curses, when his warp and woof got into some particularly intractable tangle. He did not take naturally to the weaver's craft; and the rugs and lengths of tapestry which he produced

155

were uniformly hideous; but he was a kindly fellow and saw that his compliance gave both his wife and her aunt considerable gratification; so he persevered.

But this success did not, curiously enough, satisfy Aunt Susan; although he had exchanged writing for weaving, Simon remained essentially the same bland, easy-going, unassailable character, and she felt that her remedy had proved merely cosmetic; the real deep-down problem was still untouched. So she now extended her campaign to include his gardening activities.

"There's something very *obsessional*, don't you think, about the way you mow and mow that lawn?" she said to Simon.

"The grass grows uncommonly fast in June," he pointed out.

"Ah, but don't you *see*, my dear boy, the motives go much deeper than you realize. All that cutting—clipping—pruning —hoeing—slashing—chopping that you do—can't you see what it is really aimed at?"

"The garden," said Simon.

"The garden is only a symbol. Can't you grasp that concept? Don't you see whom the garden really represents?"

"No, I can't say that I do."

"Your mother!" said Aunt Susan triumphantly. "All this violence inflicted on the garden is really the manifestation of profound feelings of hostility (and consequent guilt) towards your mother."

"But she's dead."

"That makes no difference. That only makes it more complicated, because she isn't there in person, and you have to take it out on the garden. Just look how short you cut those borders!"

"That was so I wouldn't have to do them again for ten days."

156

"No, Simon dear, you were really attacking your mother, because when you were a child she used to wash your face and scold you, and make you finish the fat on your meat, and go to bed when you'd rather stay up."

"Actually," said Simon, thinking it over, "I was pretty fond of my Ma. She was a great one for larks—we used to have a lot of good times when I was a boy."

"Ah! That's what you *think*! But deep down—buried, almost forgotten—you will find there are all kinds of other memories—of struggles, anger, rage and hatred. Now what you must do is stop gardening for a few months and try, really try *hard*, to recall all those unresolved conflicts. You will be truly surprised at what a difference it will make!"

"Oh yes, darling, *do* try!" said Delia, who was beginning to be won round to Aunt Susan's point of view, since she heard it morning, noon and night.

So for two months Simon stopped his gardening activities, and merely sat in the greenhouse, trying to remember forgotten quarrels with his mother.

The first result of this was that the garden became overgrown with enormous weeds. But Simon manfully ignored them, wrestling with his obdurate subconscious, which continued to refuse to yield any memories of familial conflict. What it did produce, instead, night after night, were a number of remarkably vivid dreams, which he would relate at breakfast.

"I dreamed that I saw you drowning again, Aunt Susan. This time it wasn't in the sea, but in a huge jar of Golden Syrup. The syrup had just reached your chin when I woke up."

"That's excellent—extremely satisfactory," Aunt Susan responded with great cordiality. "You are really beginning to co-operate. The dream shows a repressed wish to murder

Delia; all husbands wish to murder their wives at some point in the marriage."

"Oh? Then why should I dream that it is *you* who are drowning?"

"You see, you are using me as a substitute-figure. The subconscious always prefers to conceal its real impulses."

By now August had come, and Simon suggested a picnic by the sea.

Unfortunately, while Simon and Aunt Susan were dozing after the picnic lunch, Delia, who adored bathing, swam an injudicious distance out to sea, was seized by cramps, and drowned before she could be rescued. Everybody knew what a devoted couple the young Caraways had been; the deepest sympathy was expressed by the Coroner and all Simon's friends.

But Aunt Susan said: "I'm afraid, Simon dear, that poor Delia must have absorbed *too deeply* the knowledge of your subconscious wish to drown her. I am not saying that she deliberately committed suicide—dear Delia was too strong, too brave a character to do such a thing as that—but the awareness of your feelings *must* have contributed to her mental and physical state. Those cramps will have been a psychosomatic response to that knowledge. It is something that you will just have to learn to live with, I am afraid."

"No," said Simon, "for once you are wrong, Aunt Susan."

"How do you mean, my dear boy? You cannot seriously be suggesting that Delia killed herself?"

"No, indeed I am not. I put two tablespoonfuls of powdered glass into her hard-boiled egg sandwich. That was what gave her the cramps."

"*Simon!* You must be joking! You can't mean what you say?"

"No, I am perfectly serious," said Simon. "I began to see

158

that, if your theories were correct, drowning Delia would appear to be the only solution to my problem."

"*What*?!!!"

"The only difficulty," he went on, "is that now I find drowning Delia was evidently *not* the solution."

"What do you mean?" Aunt Susan asked with chattering teeth.

"Why, because of my dreams! I still keep dreaming about *your* death, Aunt Susan. Only now the death has changed its form. I keep dreaming that you are being smothered in a handwoven rug. And what," inquired Simon, picking up a large hideous handwoven rug which he had recently completed, and advancing on his wife's aunt in a decidedly menacing manner, "what do you suggest that I should do about that, Aunt Susan?"

Acknowledgements

"Wing Quack Flap" was first published in *Cold Feet* (Hodder & Stoughton 1985); "Homer's Whistle" was in *They Wait* (Pepper Press 1983); and "The Blades" was in *Out of Time* (Bodley Head 1984).